MICHAEL RIDDING

A DENCOM THRILLER

S.T. HOOVER

This is a work of fiction. Characters, companies, organizations and agencies in this novel are either the product of the author's imagination or, if real, used fictitiously without any intent to describe their actual conduct. Any and all resemblance to persons, living or dead, is entirely coincidental.

"Hand holding Gun (with glove + silencer)" image found at: http://www.officialpsds.com/Hand-holding-Gun-with-glove--silencer-PSD67729.html
Used with Creative Commons Attribution 3.0 Unported License. Edited from original image to blend with cover.

MICHAEL RIDDING

A DENCOM THRILLER

S.T. Hoover

For Dad

"HUMANITY HAS RISEN BEYOND THE CONFINES OF PERCEPTIBLE REALITY THROUGH THE ART OF CONSPIRACY AND MYSTERY. Properly executed, the search for something greater has always led to advancement, be the initial hypothesis proven true or false. If the urge to know more, to find something greater than ourselves, was not present, mankind would still be swimming around the ocean, accepting of the deep, endless blue as the only reality.

"But we didn't. We went to the surface and found a new level of existence, as humanity always tries to do. It is a trait that has led to what should have been a simple, ignorant species, unaware of its own creation and creator, gaining collective will beyond basic instinct.

"If the search for more were to end, humanity would be stunted in its continuing growth, left to only ponder the greater meaning, to grow cold inside as belief in something greater than itself fades away, taking free will and consciousness with it.

"This, my friend, would mark the end of the world."

-M.P.
Just Beyond the Surface, Waiting on the Beach.

1

Tuesday, July 23rd
Irvine Spectrum Shopping Mall
Irvine, California
3:47 PM

HE SAT ALONE IN THE WAITING AREA OF THE OPEN-AIR MALL IN ONE OF THE MANY WOODEN CHAIRS. The blue fabric awning of Dave and Buster's made the bright midday sun and hundred-degree temperatures tolerable.

In front of him was a small, simple black table. His untouched lemonade sat in the center, a growing pool of condensation ringed around the bottom. He held a large smartphone in a leather flip case, responding to messages from his store manager.

He was wearing a pair of Robert Wayne loafers, an older pair from a long dead line that he prided himself in having acquired. They were adorned with an abstract seal, the design reminiscent of an ancient islander's artistic take on a crocodile. His button-up dress shirt slowly faded from red to black, finally matching his black dress pants.

Michael Ridding, named after his grandfather, didn't look like he wanted to be bothered.

At thirty-six, he stood six-foot-three with an intimidating face to most. However, those who knew him well only saw it as inviting. His thick brown hair was combed and slicked to his right side, several bleached patches barely visible as his natural color consumed them.

A ringing suddenly filled his left ear, and he reached up to correct the issue. He'd worn a hearing aid the majority of his life and always hated the things. In his youth, they were large, indiscreet units plagued by constant malfunctions. Nowadays, they were barely visible and only squealed on occasion, so he tolerated the minor annoyances.

Michael looked down at the clock on his phone. He'd been sitting for just over fifteen minutes, much longer than he had planned. Usually, he would have gone off shopping to his heart's content, but it would have been rude to leave his friend and roommate at the restaurant without letting him know.

Aron Sanderson, who was still enjoying his time in the game room, was Michael's lifelong friend and now roommate. They had been inseparable since they met in elementary school, back when their families lived in Sacramento. They had gone through school together, drudged their way through college in Ohio, then found themselves living not far apart when Michael moved to Palm Springs after managing an aquarium import facility in Dallas.

After Aron lost his home to a wildfire back in May, Michael had let him move in. How long their arrangement would last, Michael didn't know, but they were content for the short term. Having someone to talk over the work day with was something neither of them knew they missed. In truth, Michael hoped Aron would live with him for as long as possible. Otherwise, it would just be him and the cat again, and however much comfort Granger was, she wasn't exactly the best listener.

He set the phone down. Sipping his lemonade, he watched the shoppers come and go, most of them groups of young people migrating from one fashion store to another like schools of fish on a reef.

The minutes continued to tick by with no sign of Aron. Michael didn't worry; odds were, Aron had gotten carried away.

Again.

Normally reserved, when given the chance he would branch out and have some fun. Michael had left him at the skee ball lanes, where he was challenging some kid to see who could get the highest score. It was good-natured fun, but Michael was looking forward to the day when Aron realized how immature he looked. Compared to his best friend, Aron had always been a little less uptight, but the last few years had seen Aron break out of his shell more often. Michael supposed it had something to do with the job.

Michael couldn't help but reflect on his work. The excursion to the Spectrum was meant to be a cool-down after a long, tedious meeting with their boss while he had been in town. Instead, Michael could feel the sun creeping over the protection of the awning as it lowered, threatening to take his remaining patience with it across the hazy blue sky.

He drew his thoughts inward, letting go of his concerns about Aron. He found himself looking back to the time when his life had taken a dramatic turn. A turn that led him to this moment.

He let the memory consume him, oblivious to the three men getting ready to kill him just out of sight.

2

LIFE AFTER COLLEGE HAD BEEN DIFFICULT FOR MICHAEL.

Shortly after graduation, he moved to Dallas and worked for a tropical fish distribution center. After spending two years making a good living off of something he loved, things took a turn. He suffered something his parents had feared and predicted: A quarter-life crisis.

Desperate to make something more of his life, he saved enough to lease a condo in Palm Springs and started his own aquarium shop, Modern Aquaria. Initially, the shop did well, winning over most of the local aquarium enthusiasts and drawing new people into the hobby. Years later, though, hard times hit nationwide, and aquariums became a luxury few could afford. The shop did worse and worse over time, much to his disappointment. After months of struggling to keep the shop going, Michael was forced to announce that the store was closing.

That was when Benedict found him.

If Michael had a list of the oddest people he had ever

met in his life, Benedict would have soared to the top on psychotic wings.

It was the final week of business and Michael was working alone, catering to no one when an unfamiliar face walked into the shop. He was a younger, slightly heavy man who was just shorter than Michael. He wore a long, black wool coat in the hundred-and-six-degree heat. Black denim pants and black dress shoes peeked out from underneath the coat, and Michael could make out a white T-shirt and a black, rectangular pendant around the man's neck.

"Hey there," Michael said, welcoming the man as he did all customers.

But the smaller man appeared intimidated, initially drawing back before returning the welcome with a nod and forced smile. He started browsing and was soon lost among the rows of aquariums and supplies.

Looking back, Michael could never place why, but he had felt that now more than ever would be a good time to check the security cameras. Using a system of his own design, he turned on the monitors, knowing that any obvious robbery would be caught on the DVR back in his office. The monitor, hidden under the cashier's desk, took a moment to warm up before the multi-image screen displayed the four security camera feeds.

He saw the man in aisle four among the tanks of saltwater livestock, hunched over and...

Is he crying?

Michael saw the slow heaving of the man's chest and

the constant wiping of his eyes. He was obviously upset, and he was trying to hide it.

In the otherwise empty store, Michael could hear the man talking to himself, his voice barely audible over the buzzing and bubbling aquarium filters.

"You *have* to. You *need* to," he was saying. "You came all this way, came this far. You can't throw it away now that you know what he *means.*"

The man's head shot up, searching to see if he had been heard, oblivious to the hidden security camera among the décor across from him.

Now, Michael could clearly make out the man's face. His eyes were red and his cheeks were pink from wiping away tears. He looked down, making more of an effort to compose himself.

Michael tensed. The man could be some kind of nut-bag or drug addict—or worse. He had come across some before; Palm Springs was known for its diversity and acceptance of alternative lifestyles—most of which were accepted and even encouraged—but it was no longer the most "family-friendly" place, once one searched behind the blacked-out windows of supposedly abandoned buildings. Every once in a while, some "undesirables" would creep out from those dark buildings and into the light when least expected. They were far from welcome, even in the famously tolerant city.

Was this man one of them?

3

MICHAEL GAZED DOWN AT HIS SCREEN. The smaller man steadied himself on the aquarium shelves with his right hand. As he watched, the man's face slowly returned to its normal color. It had been five minutes since the man had spoken out loud, and Michael was certain he was about to make his move. Whatever that was.

Michael had no weapon. Not because he had anything against them, but because he simply didn't think he needed one. However, he suddenly wished he had a gun within reach as he saw the man approach the counter.

As he rounded the corner, Michael saw that he wore that same forced smile.

"Mr. Ridding," the man began as he came up to the desk and extended a hand. "My name is Benedict, and if you don't mind, I would like to take a moment of your time to talk about a business proposal."

How did this strange man know his name? Was he some old contact, maybe a sales representative from one of the various companies he stocked? Maybe they had met at a trade show? It was possible, but then again, this was someone Michael knew he would have remembered.

Even so, he sounded as awkward as a young kid reading in front of a class. The presentation was obviously rehearsed, but there was genuine passion in the forced words. Whatever this guy wanted to talk over, he was serious, but also unsure of how to handle the situation. Michael considered the request. If it was a legitimate proposal, he was willing to hear it, but why present him with this now when the store was about to close?

Finally given a better chance to look the man over, Michael reconsidered his earlier assessment. It was obvious that Benedict wasn't a drug addict or some other undesirable.

To start with, he smelled good. He wore a copious amount of Oxford Bleu cologne, the distinct scent crossing the distance between them with ease. His well-tailored coat was nicely set and freshly cleaned—not a hair clung to it.

It was like Michael was talking to a completely different man than the one who had walked in.

Michael grasped the outstretched hand while glancing at his wristwatch. It was just after twelve-thirty. "Well, I was about to close for lunch, so I guess we can talk in the break room, if you like."

Benedict made little attempt to contain his joy.

Michael flipped the "Closed" sign, not bothering to lock the door, and showed Benedict to the small employee lunch area. The room consisted of a microwave atop a mini-fridge and a round folding table with two matching chairs. Michael let Benedict have a seat first, then walked to the refrigerator.

"You want anything? We have burritos, soup?"

"No thanks, I ate on the plane," Benedict said, then quickly grew quiet, as if he'd been silently reprimanded.

"Well, I hope you don't mind if I have something. It'll be my first meal all day." Or perhaps his only meal, but he didn't tell Benedict that. If this man was here to discuss business, it wasn't in his best interest to imply that he barely had enough money for one microwaved meal a day. "So, you just flew in?"

"Yeah, my plane came in just a couple hours ago. I had a layover and thought I would stop in town," Benedict said as Michael put his food in the microwave.

"Well, feel free to let me know if I'm keeping you," Michael said.

"Oh, they won't leave without me," Benedict said uncomfortably, as if he wasn't sure if he should be saying anything at all.

"Wish airlines would do that for me," Michael remarked. He hadn't flown in a long time. Even then, it had been for business, and he found none of the sparse trips to trade shows enjoyable.

"Well, they have to, since it's my plane," Benedict said with a hint of resistance.

Michael looked back, his eyes bulging. "You have your own *plane*?"

"Well, I wouldn't call it *mine*. It's the company's private jet, but I have priority," Benedict replied.

Michael fought to keep his jaw from dropping. Benedict's claim of having a private jet left him surprised, yet troubled. It seemed impossible that any company with the resources to maintain such an asset would be interested in *his* small shop.

The microwave went off and Michael retrieved his meal.

"All right," he said, cautiously walking to the table and sitting across from Benedict. "You have my attention."

4

"WHAT I'M ABOUT TO SAY IS LUDICROUSLY STUPID," BENEDICT BEGAN, "BUT I ASK THAT YOU KEEP AN OPEN MIND. If you have any questions, I can answer them after."

Michael nodded for Benedict to continue.

The flood of information the man let loose was overwhelming, but Michael kept quiet until the end.

"About a year ago, I came into possession of an extensive communications and networking corporation. Known as DenCom to most of the public, its advanced technologies division currently supplies the United States with the majority of its newest tech. Flight systems, satellites, even a few aircraft are in the works.

"I got to know the old CEO about a year before taking over the company. He'd heard about me through... okay, I know how stupid this is gonna sound, but he heard about me through my... 'exploits' in cryptozoology. I was job-hunting in Florida when he asked me to visit Denver, my old hometown. I accepted his offer, and he paid for a first-class ticket.

"I was taken straight from the airport to a house close by the Rockies. There, I was led to the bed of an old man who told me his name was Herbert Morecraft. He'd heard about the hobbies I had in my youth—ghost-hunting, UFOs, all that kind of stuff. Nothing ever came of it, though, until I was out of high school and I camped out in the Sierra Nevadas to look for Sasquatch. As I'm sure you've already assumed, I was young and stupid, so I got lost pretty quickly.

"As far as I was concerned, the trip was a complete failure. I was lost out there for three months with nothing but my coat and survival guide. I panicked, went feral, turned into a mountain man eating berries and catching trout out of streams to survive. Eventually, some hikers found me and took me back to town.

"After I got out of the hospital, I decided I'd had enough excitement for one lifetime. I spent four years in Seattle getting a useless degree in business management, then spent another year looking for work, living out of my car and cheap hotels so I could stay mobile. Near the end of that year was when Morecraft interviewed me.

"He told me two things. One, his doctors told him he was dying and he had less than a year to live, and two, that he'd researched me and was hoping I could take over as the new CEO once he passed away. I was *floored*. He laughed, then offered me a deal.

"He offered to fund a full expedition for the Sasquatch with me as the team leader. We could spend the next six months going wherever we wanted and doing whatever we wanted, but if we could prove the creature's existence, then I would have fulfilled my end of the bargain, and he would sign over DenCom to me. He also said that if I did become CEO, he wanted me to pick up where he left off on his own investigations after he was gone. What could I say to that? He was offering me a chance to pursue my—albeit strange—passion. Plus, he offered me a hefty paycheck whether I came back with proof or not, just for my time. So, I accepted his offer, and here I am."

Michael took the story in. It was obviously rehearsed, but much of it sounded sincere. *But what was the point?*

He'd never been a believer in the paranormal, apart from the existence of ghosts. In his youth he saw things, most of them probably figments of his imagination. Nonetheless, the experiences had opened the door to research in the phenomena, and he came out a believer. But everything else that fell under the catch-all term of "paranormal" didn't particularly interest him. Still, his curiosity was piqued.

"So you found one?" Michael asked cautiously.

"Well, I'm CEO, so I must have found something," Benedict answered with a hint of sarcasm.

"All right, then what did you find? A live one? Footprints? Hair?"

"If I could tell you, I would, but one of the things Morecraft and I agreed on was that none of the discoveries I made using his resources could become public. I mean, couldn't you just see hillbilly gangs heading up into the woods and killing every last one if they knew where to look?"

Michael opened his mouth to answer, but before he could, Benedict continued.

"Before he died, Morecraft said he wanted me to bring in more people to help me in my work. He didn't name anyone in particular, but in my..." Benedict trailed off, gathering his thoughts. Several tense moments passed before he continued, "In my research, you and your friend Aron both showed up as potential candidates. Don't ask why because honestly, I don't quite know myself. I'm simply trusting the judgment of those who advise me."

Michael raised an eyebrow.

"I want to offer you a deal, Michael. If you agree to help me with my research and expeditions, I will see to it that your store stays open. Not only that, but you will be paid generously to investigate and research a variety of subjects, from paranormal to political to religious. It's all totally legal and sanctioned by the US government, as long as we do the occasional side work for them, in addition to giving them any valuable finds from our own investigations. I'm not allowed to answer the 'why' questions about your projects—or even say if your work is a success in some cases—but I can say you will make a good living and find fulfillment with the work you do. If at any time, that isn't true, just let me know, and we *will* fix that. The arrangement would benefit everyone. I really, *really* think we can make this work."

As Benedict caught his breath, Michael let the first of several questions out of his head. "You want me to take a second job working for you, and in exchange, you'll pay me and support my shop?"

"Yep." Benedict looked relieved, as if an enormous weight had been lifted from his shoulders.

"And I'll have no idea what I'm working on until you tell me?"

"In some cases, yes. Think of it like you're working alone on one corner of a puzzle. You may not know what it is—and I may not either—but when everyone puts their corners together, we get a picture. If you don't feel like it's a good fit..." he trailed off, his breathing still heavy. "If it's not a good fit, then we can work something out. Plus, like I said, if your own interests are desirable and could provide useful results, I would be more than happy to let you pursue them with our help."

Michael thought he would have more to ask, but as Benedict caught his breath, only one more question escaped his lips: "How do I know this isn't a scam?"

Benedict reached into his coat pocket and produced a large packet that Michael was surprised could have been concealed without being noticed. He placed it on the table, taking one long look at it before sliding it across to Michael.

"Everything you'll need to convince yourself is in there. I think it would be best if you took a day or two to look it over before making your choice. There's a card with my personal phone number on it, so when the time comes to say yes or no, call me. Everything else should be self-explanatory." Benedict got up and pushed his chair in. "I may not be reachable for the next twelve hours or so. Where I'm heading, I don't get great reception. By tomorrow morning, though, I should be able to take calls."

Benedict extended a hand to Michael, who hesitated for a moment before shaking. Part of him hoped that whatever was inside the packet was bogus and that the whole thing turned out to be a scam. He knew there could be dark things down that path, things he didn't want to get involved in. And as he looked into Benedict's eyes for the last time that day, he thought he could see what that kind of research could do to someone.

They ended the handshake, and Benedict headed for the door. "Think it over and give me a call. And for the moment, don't tell anyone, not even Aron until I can talk to him personally." He gave a small wave. "I'll see you in time."

Benedict left the break room, and shortly after, Michael heard the front door chime, signaling his departure.

Benedict had put on a good show, but he still could have been a brilliant con artist. It could all be a game, an elaborate plot meant to take everything Michael had left, which was already dwindling dangerously close to nothing by the day.

Money was so tight, he was considering talking to his parents again and seeing if he could move back home to Sacramento for a while. It was a prospect he loathed, mostly since it had been over a year since he had spoken with them. They hadn't approved of his choice to leave Dallas, and the few times they had talked since the move had been tense, to say the least. When it came to his father, who never failed to bring it up, "hostile" would have been a better word. He knew he was a disappointment to them, forgoing relationships and stability in favor of his own desires.

Now, he might have an opportunity to do things right in their eyes, but he couldn't say he wanted to.

He left the packet on the table and headed for the computer. First, he looked up DenCom and found it was an actual corporation. Not only that, but it was indeed the leader in non-commercial tech for businesses and the US government. He also found out that since the company's founding in the sixties, no one had ever gotten an interview with either CEO, but he found purported pictures of them on conspiracy sites. Apparently, Morecraft and Benedict's work had not gone unnoticed by those in tinfoil hats.

He found an article on one site detailing Morecraft's disappearance and Benedict's arrival onto the scene. The article included pictures of who they thought were the two CEOs. The older man in the first picture wore thick glasses and a slightly disheveled tan tweed sports jacket. Michael could tell the picture was likely taken without Morecraft's knowledge, since he wasn't looking at the camera and a blurry cityscape could be seen behind him. The other picture was obviously of Benedict, who also seemed oblivious to the photographer. His coat was blowing in the wind, and he looked to be on an airport tarmac with two other, much taller men: One was bald, the other sported a short Mohawk.

The article itself was essentially useless. It was a lot of "We know something is going on. We don't know what, but *something*!"

He closed the computer, only slightly less cautious

about the situation. Benedict was the subject of some crackpot's mystery article. So what? Couldn't that crackpot be Benedict himself, just another layer of the man's scheme? He obviously knew Michael was going to look him up, so could he have written the article?

At least DenCom existed. That was verifiable. In fact, as he thought back to his last trip to Denver for a trade show, he had seen DenCom Tower in person. It was the largest building in the city, standing easily a third taller than the rest.

On top of that, it seemed well-established that the CEO had never been a public figure, and that he was only known by his first name, even within the company. Still, the article implied that the name might have been taken from the recently renamed street that led to DenCom Tower: Benedict Street.

He'd seen enough. He had to open the packet.

Michael headed back to the break room, the packet still lying on the table. He opened it, flipped it over, and let three items fall out. The first was a plain white business card with Benedict's number written on it. The second was an employee manual that was easily an inch thick, labeled *Practice and Procedure for DenCom Private Agents*. Michael flipped through it, paying little attention to the text.

The third item was a small envelope labeled "Advance" in rushed handwriting. He gently opened it and nearly fell out of his chair.

Inside was a check made out to him for a million

dollars.

5

"WELL, I'M GLAD YOU DIDN'T LEAVE WITHOUT ME."

Michael retreated from the memory to find Aron standing beside him, grinning as he sported a large, furry red dragon under his left arm. Michael looked over his disheveled friend. His bright blond hair, normally slicked to the left side, was messy and out of place. His light turquoise shirt was pressed to his skinny frame by a fresh sheen of sweat.

Michael hadn't expected anything less. He took another glance at the red dragon.

"What the hell is that?"

"I won it," Aron explained. "They didn't have any prizes I wanted and I thought your brother's kids might enjoy it."

Mark, Michael's older brother, was not someone he saw often, but he and Aron always hit it off. Mark was a nice enough guy, but he was also an idiot: He had married the only girl he ever dated and now, they had three kids in Apple Valley. However, Mark and his wife seemed happy, and the kids adored their uncle and Aron, so Michael kept his mouth shut.

"Great idea, I'll see when he's—" Michael began before he was cut off by a curse escaping Aron's lips.

The dragon hit the ground softly, letting out a roar from its voice box as it came to rest on its side. Aron bent down, complaining about losing his grip, when something else caught Michael's eye.

The pillar behind Aron erupted outward from a small hole at eye level. As pebbles settled at their feet, Michael realized too late what had happened.

As Michael turned to examine the cavity, his right shoulder was sharply thrown back, pushing him to the ground with a smack as his head connected with the brick walkway.

Then, he felt the hot, searing pain of a bullet wound and blood seeping out beneath him.

Screaming filled the air. Several people rushed to help him, but they scattered as a man nearby took a third bullet to the head. He fell to his knees, shattered skull fragments caving in as he knelt. Then, he fell face-first onto the ground, and gravity finished the job. His head deflated like a battered balloon.

Aron rushed to help Michael, only to be cut off by a stream of silenced gunfire that made him retreat behind the pillar.

With all the strength he could find, Michael forced himself up and hobbled across to the opposite pillar while the unseen gunmen's view was blocked by the fleeing crowds.

"Aron, go!" Michael ordered as he slumped beside the pillar, just barely able to stand.

Aron didn't move. He looked to the doors of Dave and Buster's only a few feet away, then back to Michael.

"Go! Get help!" Michael roared over the crowds. He could see the doubt in Aron's eyes. Who was there to call? It was a poor distraction, but he wouldn't be able to live with himself if he let Aron die in an attempt to save him. "I'll be fine!"

Reluctantly, Aron sprinted to the entrance, bullets striking around his feet as he burst through the doors and out of sight.

Michael felt at least some relief as Aron disappeared, but the sensation was soon replaced by crippling panic.

More screams echoed through the mall. More gunfire as countless innocent people were killed. What the hell was this? A terrorist attack? But why here? Why him and Aron? He tried to contain his questions and bottle up his fear as he told himself to think logically about his next step.

In the end, instinct prevailed.

As shoppers fled to one of three walkways leaving the food court, Michael joined them. Hidden among the crowd, he followed the flow of panicked traffic in a hasty retreat.

He caught a brief glimpse of one of the terrorists sidestepping from behind a sunglass kiosk, shooting as he went. Several people in front of him collapsed. One man, dead before he had hit the ground, suddenly blocked his escape.

Toppling over the bleeding corpse, Michael landed hands-first, cushioning the rest of his body before he crumpled under the stampede of panicked shoppers. The air left his lungs as he felt his body sinking into the ground, the steady flow of feet against his back restricting his airflow. As the screams of the crowd faded away, Michael sensed what was coming next.

6

MICHAEL OPENED A WEAK EYE TO SEE TWO MEN RACING TOWARD HIM. Both wore white polo shirts and sported muscular figures that revealed they either worked out rigorously or took a lot of steroids. Michael presumed the latter.

Guns fixed on him, they slowed to a cautious stop. He didn't know if they thought he was dead or not, but he was obviously of interest to them.

"Erickson," one of the men said, lowering his weapon. "You didn't wait for the go-ahead!"

Out of sight, Michael could hear the approaching footsteps of another man, but didn't want to risk taking a look. The man came to a stop only inches from his head, inserting a new magazine with a metallic click as he did so.

"Doesn't matter. I think we did just fine," the man behind him said. Michael felt the cold barrel of the gun pressed against his head. "Father will be proud."

Before Michael had the chance to panic, the gun was removed from his temple. The man behind him stood up and walked past him swiftly, gun raised toward the sky, and joined the other two identical men.

"What the hell is it?" the one called Erickson asked.

Moments passed, Michael silently questioning why he wasn't shot as the three gunmen tried to figure something out.

As some senses came back to him, Michael heard a loud crash and a car engine that sounded vaguely familiar.

The gunmen walked on, leaving Michael to contemplate the growing roar. Once they were out of sight, he risked taking a look.

He did so just as his black 1973 Pantera rounded the wide corner with Aron at the wheel.

Michael didn't dare move as the three men unloaded on the windshield. Aron ducked as bullets reduced the glass to microscopic shards. Dozens of bullets struck the hood and interior without any sign of letting up.

The barrage was short lived.

The Pantera barreled into the three men, the roar of gunfire replaced with the snap of bones as the car bounced up a small stairway, the angled front bumper meeting each man just above the hip.

They flew over Michael, their bodies soaring limply past. All three landed with a loud, deep thud, then fell still.

The car stopped just in front of Michael. Aron ran from the driver's side and helped Michael stand, then quickly ushered him into the passenger's seat. He brushed off as much glass as possible before letting Michael sit down.

"Benedict..." Michael said weakly as Aron got back in the driver's seat. "Call... Benedict."

"As soon as we get to the Irvine office," Aron said. "They have a private garage where we can hide the car until things calm down. Where do you hurt?"

"Just... everywhere," Michael managed as he began to drift out of consciousness. The statement, despite sounding sarcastic, was far too accurate. His ribs and gut hurt the most—next to his ruined shoulder, of course. And yet, it was getting harder to feel anything. The pain began to fade as he drifted away.

Except his breathing. It still hurt to breathe.

"How's the wound?" Aron asked, speeding up as they left the deserted mall behind.

"Passed... I think it passed..."

"Just stick around a little longer. We should be there in a second."

The Irvine offices were already visible as a pair of large white buildings, the office situated near the top of the closest. Michael and Aron had met Benedict there only hours before to discuss their latest investigations.

During the meeting, Michael had seen the shopping mall from the window and thought it would be the perfect place to unwind. He laughed out loud at the thought while the door to the underground parking garage opened, consuming them in orange light as Michael drifted out of consciousness.

7

MICHAEL WOKE ENGULFED IN A BRILLIANT WHITE LIGHT. A

feminine form stared down at him, silhouetted against the haze. As the world became clearer and his senses returned, Michael made out the white garb of the nurse along with Aron, who came into view opposite her.

"Rise and shine, Mr. Ridding," the nurse said. "I can raise the head of the bed up if you want. Might make it easier for you to take your call."

"Call?" Michael asked as he focused on her slim figure. She was a small woman, barely two thirds his size. He watched her work daintily over a clipboard, waiting for clarification.

"Yes," she explained "You're not seriously hurt. The bullet wound was from a small caliber weapon, and our doctors were able to patch it up easily. Benedict is insisting that you be released soon, but he would like to talk with you first."

Before Michael could question her further, Aron cut in.

"We're still in Irvine, at a DenCom emergency medical office and care center."

Michael chuckled. "So, he doesn't even trust hospitals?"

Those who were close to Benedict knew he was not very trusting of... well, anything. His cleaners, meals, travel accommodations... almost everything Benedict needed came only from a group of trusted sources that were usually shell companies he owned. Similar to how Michael and Benedict were joint owners of Modern Aquaria, some were extra eyes and ears in the world, while others had no secrets to hide.

"You're right about that one," the nurse admitted. "Anyway, you'll have some minor pain from the wound, along with some bruising in your midsection and back. You'll ache for a while, but it should pass within a few days. If I were you, I would try to spend a couple days in bed when you get home. If possible."

Michael noticed the way she phrased everything: It was exactly how Benedict would want things to be handled. Nothing forced, no holding him down, even for his own well-being. In any other hospital, he would have been required to stay overnight for an observation period, at the very least. But that wasn't Benedict's way, and he paid people enough to respect that.

"Anyway, I don't want to leave you in a hurry, but Benedict insisted that you call him when you woke up. If it's okay, I'll grab the phone, and then you can be sent home," the nurse said.

Michael nodded.

As she left the room, Michael looked to Aron. "Is it bad?"

"Nope, you're good. You're gonna hurt like hell, but not for too long," he explained.

"I meant the Spectrum. What happened?"

Aron took a moment to respond. "They got all three men; they're completely out of it and in a secure hospital. The car's banged up, but Benedict said he would take care of-"

"How many people, Aron?" Michael cut in harshly.

Aron's response was slow and thoughtful. "Ten, all men. Five others in critical condition. Also men."

"What about—?" The nurse came in, interrupting Michael by handing him the phone and telling him it was already ringing. She was gone before the phone reached his ear, only half a ring sounding before Benedict's voice came over the line.

"Michael, ya there?" the firm, yet nervous voice asked.

"Yeah, just woke up."

"Good, good. So how are you holding up?"

Michael went over his condition and provided his supervisor with a play-by-play of the attack as he remembered it. Minutes passed as he tried to recall every detail, drawing on every bit of his seven years of experience working for DenCom. As he wrapped up, he couldn't help feeling he hadn't said enough, but Benedict seemed satisfied.

"I've spent the last few hours on and off the phone

with Robinson. He said you and Aron should be good to go home without any interference from the law. He understood you both acted in self-defense and the defense of those around you, and since he still owes me a few favors, that was all I needed to tell him. He may not be happy with how you did it, but you got the job done."

Benedict's explanation calmed Michael, but it was not unexpected. Benedict had cleared the names of many investigators who had apparently done stupid things in the name of DenCom, most of which he called "favors from the big man." Still, Michael couldn't help but feel nervous about the arrangement, mostly because he feared that one day, Benedict's favors would run out.

"That's great, but, Benedict, those guys were shooting at *us*. This wasn't some random attack. Why would they want *us* dead? Could this be about Antarctica?" Michael asked.

Antarctica had been their last investigation abroad. About a year ago, Benedict had claimed to know the location of a relic with tremendous religious value. The three of them, along with a small crew, took to the Antarctic Sea on a chartered boat, setting a course for the mainland. The mission had fallen apart after an unidentified group forced them off the continent, leaving everyone with more questions than answers. It had become clear they weren't going any further when Benedict returned to the ship, ordered them to turn around, and spent the majority of the trip back to Tasmania locked in his cabin. Supposedly, Benedict was looking into who had interrupted their expedition, but as far as Michael knew, nothing had come from it in the year since they left the frozen wasteland behind.

"I wouldn't think so. If I had to guess... maybe someone in the government doesn't like us? Could also be some of those conspiracy nuts who are always on the company's tail, but none of them have violent tendencies —at least, as far as I know..." It was clear that Benedict was sorting through all possibilities.

Seven years ago, Michael never would have been able to think like an "investigator", but his time with DenCom had gradually increased his mental stamina. It was hard at first, but with Benedict's help, he was getting better year after year at figuring out the myriad of mysteries. Still, nothing he'd done could have suggested that he and Aron would become targets. Nothing they had done could have warranted anything beyond harsh criticism or vague threats from people who had no power to back up their words.

But could this really be one of the faceless nut-jobs looking to reveal the truth about DenCom? It wasn't an entirely unreasonable possibility, but what were the odds that three of them would band together and try to take out a pair of investigators in broad daylight? Whoever had done this was greedy, wanted to hit DenCom hard and didn't care how they did so.

In the process, they had killed ten men, and perhaps five others. *But why were they so sloppy?* It didn't make sense. Michael tried to quiet his cluttered head, turning his attention back to Benedict.

"Okay, so what do we do now?"

"Well, as for me, I'm gonna lie in bed, eat some buffalo wings, and watch anime until I pass out. Tomorrow, I'll fly back to California and meet you guys around noon so we can go over all this."

Michael fought the urge to lash out at Benedict's casual response. They'd nearly been killed, and his boss was going to binge watch cartoons? Forcing himself to chalk his anger up to confusion and stress, he let it go, for now. Still, he wanted a better answer.

"But what about me and Aron?" he asked.

"Do what I'm going to: Relax. The three steroid stooges are on death's doormat, so even if they do pull through, it's not like we're getting answers from them anytime soon. For the moment, we have nothing to go on, so just try and feel better. I'll have you guys driven back tonight and the Pantera fixed up in a few days."

Michael didn't like it, but he had to admit that most of what Benedict said was right. They had nothing concrete until the FBI report was done. His body also agreed with Benedict's recommendation to destress; it had been a long, hard day. The memory of watching those innocent people die would haunt him forever, but he couldn't let anything distract him from figuring this out. He didn't want to relax, he wanted to be out there, to find out why these people wanted him dead. But he knew it was wrong to go against Benedict. Years ago, when he thought the strange man was a con artist, he couldn't have been more wrong. He was smarter and wiser than he looked and acted, and he had always been there to help them. He trusted his investigators, and his investigators trusted him.

Even if he told them to do nothing.

"So all we can do is wait?" Michael asked.

"That about sums it up, yeah," Benedict said. "I don't like it either, but it won't do any good to get our thongs in a bunch. Just feel better so we can be ready to face whatever comes next. Promise?"

Michael sighed; even though he didn't agree with Benedict, Michael knew he was probably the only one thinking clearly right now. "Fine, I'll try and relax."

"All right. I'll try and be at your place at noon," Benedict said. "If you're feeling up to it, I may want to do our normal run around town. Who knows? It might do you some good."

"Fine by me. I should be good to walk, at least." Michael looked over to see the nurse poking her head in again, whispering something to Aron. "I think they're ready for us. See you tomorrow."

"Later," Benedict said, and they ended the call.

He set the phone on the table as Aron and the nurse came over and helped him out of bed. The three of them headed to the garage, where a new Rolls-Royce waited to take them back to Palm Springs.

8

THE DRIVE BACK WAS SPENT MOSTLY IN SILENCE, THE ONLY NOISE COMING FROM ARON'S LEAKING EAR BUDS AND THE RUSH OF WIND AS MICHAEL LOWERED THE WINDOW, LETTING HIS HAIR BLOW IN THE COOL, DRY DESERT BREEZE.

They had just passed the Morongo Casino and were almost to Michael's condo. They were just far enough from the city lights that Michael could make out a blanket of stars on the horizon. The moon was a crescent, near the end of the first half of its journey across the clear sky. It didn't get much further before the lights of Palm Springs smothered its companions again.

They reached Michael's condo just before one that night. Aron went ahead of him to check on the animals while Michael stayed behind and tipped the driver. When the driver left, Michael headed down the path through the small Birds of Paradise garden, then onto the stairs up to his second-story condo.

He could feel his legs straining, but he would never admit it to Aron. The short walk, barely a hundred feet, was getting to him. He prayed it was because of the hours he spent in bed and not something that might linger through the coming days. Clenching his teeth, he tried to maintain a casual appearance as he ascended the stairway.

The lights were beginning to turn on inside, and as he neared the door, Michael could hear Granger's purring from inside. He entered to find Aron petting the large Serval cat's head, responding to its purrs with, "Good girl. Did you miss us?"

She was at least three feet long and, two feet tall, had dangerously sharp claws, and was the biggest sweetheart of a cat either man had ever met.

Although Serval cats were generally reserved for zoos and a select few private owners who had the resources for them to live outside, Granger had never fully adjusted to zoo life. Michael had been present during her birth during one of his investigations for Benedict, and he noticed the difference right away. The week-old kitten wouldn't leave the cage she was born in, crying and wiggling violently as keepers tried to pick her up. For some reason, the only person she was remotely okay with being held by was Michael. After Michael had finished working with them and Granger was growing larger, the keepers tried to get her to adjust to living outdoors. She became sick with stress, refusing to eat or drink for nearly a week. In desperation, the lead caretaker called Michael to come over and see if he could convince her to eat. He came, and for the first time, Granger ate and drank in her new enclosure, but only while Michael was present.

Almost against his will, he began to love the animal, and against his better judgment, he agreed to take the cat for a trial run living at his home. At the time, she was only half her adult size, but she ate constantly, as if she were making up for lost time. It was a learning curve for both of them, and after some initial issues pertaining to not playing with the aquariums and the chandelier not being a good place for a nap, Granger was finally settled in and happy. Michael was allowed to keep her, as long as she reported to the vet for checkups and he brought her back to the zoo every week or so to exercise. He agreed, and the cat was doing better than any of them had expected. She was well-behaved and content with being left alone during the day, but she was still overjoyed when he and Aron came home.

As Michael shut the door, the cat left Aron's side and hurried over to him, purring and rubbing her long body against his leg. Michael gave her a pat and admitted that he missed her, as he did every day when he and Aron came home from work. He felt like sitting on the couch with her and resting, but his body strongly objected. He needed to collapse on his bed and fall asleep.

Aron called dibs on the shower, and Michael didn't protest. He was done with the day, done with trying to figure things out. But he was also feeling something else, something he thought he'd left behind at the Spectrum.

He was afraid.

9

A MILLION DOLLARS A YEAR.

Would it still be worth it?

In the darkness of the large master bedroom, the only light present was that of the large flat screen TV mounted on the wall, projecting a plethora of anime action and violence. It was all reflected on the lone pair of eyes that stared into it, lost in thought.

Benedict was not the frightened, self-conscious man he had been when he had first met Michael Ridding. Back then, the business was still new to him, and his past had yet to relinquish its hold on him. While he was no longer easily intimidated by those he had been advised to bring into his escapades, he was still worried for his own safety and sanity.

Well, maybe safety.

Most of what resembled sanity had long since faded into the far reaches of his mind, where it only came out when he deemed it necessary. The rest of the time, Benedict knew he was more or less out of control. His interests and activities clashed with what a man of his financial status was expected to be, and he feared that someday, he would succumb to the stereotype.

But that day had yet to arrive, and he prayed it never would.

On most days, the fast-paced, action-packed, breast-jiggling madness that was Benedict's favorite TV show since high school would have held his interest until, overcome by a food coma, he would drift off to sleep. But tonight, he couldn't get into the show, and he found himself doing exactly what he had told Michael and Aron not to do: Stress over the attack.

He knew Aron would be fine. For the last decade, all Aron claimed to do was relax and not dwell on mistakes or hard times. Benedict admired his friend for it, and he wished feeling the same would be that easy, especially when he was alone. He tried to emulate the practice, but it wasn't working this time.

His friends were safe, and the terrorists were in custody. But was it really so simple? He knew Michael wouldn't let this go so easily, which was the main reason why he would be flying into Palm Springs in the morning. He needed to see them again, calm them down face to face, and hopefully clear his own head in the process.

But things all over were going wrong. The meeting in Irvine was a waste of time—nothing but paperwork with Michael and Aron that led nowhere. Soon afterward, Benedict had gotten a call that one of their experimental aircraft was sighted in Utah during another test flight. In the moment or two it would have been visible, a blurry picture had been snapped. Now, it was making the rounds on UFO websites, where everyone and their mother believed that E.T. had just phoned home. At this rate, the craft would never be ready to see service, for Benedict or otherwise.

And then, as he landed, he had gotten the news about the attack. He thought it was an isolated incident until he saw the news reports and realized how serious it was. He had called Aron for an update, who told him they were both fine. He then proceeded to get their end of things straightened out, as always.

Now, it was being reported that the terrorists were in custody, and the man who drove the Pantera into them was being touted as a hero. The driver had not wanted to be named for "obvious risks to his family", and since no camera had gotten a good look at him, that appeared to be the end of it. The nation was obviously an emotional wreck, but these days, shootings happened all the time. Sadly, this one would become nothing more than a memory after the next week or so.

Until then, media coverage focused on speculation, as did Benedict. If the three men survived—which, by the hour, looked less and less likely—they would eventually talk, but they would be in far too much pain to be useful. But if Benedict got his way, *he* would be the one to interrogate them, preferably in an empty room with nothing but harsh words and a crowbar.

Still, he did fear that this could be just the beginning.

He feared losing his investigators, specifically Michael and Aron. They were valuable—necessary, even—allies, but would they want to continue working for him after something like this?

Was a million a year really enough to keep them both around, especially at the risk of losing their lives? Sure, it was a lot of money, but they couldn't use it if they were dead. Would tomorrow's meeting bring their resignations? Did he need to be prepared for that?

Something very obvious told him he didn't: Michael didn't want to go. He had been vocal about wanting to find out why his life had been put at risk, and Aron would follow Michael through Hell and back.

Whatever tomorrow held, Benedict thought he would be prepared.

He was wrong.

His cell phone came alive on the nightstand, a rooster crowing to heavy metal music blaring through the small speakers. Benedict paused the TV show and looked down at the phone.

The contact icon was a picture of Hipster Spock, the name under it simply reading: *Nelson*.

Benedict arched himself on the headboard before answering, "Nelson, it's really late."

"Three in the morning, yes—" Benedict resisted the sudden urge to swear under his breath. Was that really how late it was? "—but we have a problem with the terrorists."

Benedict was now fully awake. He knew from

Nelson's tone he wouldn't be getting any sleep after all.

"What kind of problem?"

10

Wednesday, July 24th
Kaiser Irvine Medical Center
Irvine, California
1:49 AM

DR. MALCOLM, LEAD PHYSICIAN AT KAISER IRVINE, HAD HIS HANDS FULL.

Seven gang violence victims filled rooms on the right side of the hallway, all most likely without insurance and who were probably going to die in the coming week. There was a man on the left, the most loathed of all his patients, who had taken the police on a chase down the 91 freeway and had been forced off the road to bring it to an end. He was awake, but he was locked down to his bed, with several broken limbs and massive internal damage. All he could do was curse at the top of his lungs.

Then he had three unknowns, the men from the Irvine Spectrum attack. Each where restrained to their own, separated rooms and had various spine injuries and internal issues. All three wore John Doe name tags until they were identified. As such, he couldn't offer much help or conduct possibly life-saving surgery until he had their medical backgrounds. The most he could do for now was restrain them and try to numb their pain.

Malcolm went in to check on them, as he had throughout the night. The first thing he noticed was that the lone guard they had spared to the wing was missing. This was no surprise to Malcolm; he was a young man, inexperienced and an infamous slacker. Normally, this would have upset Malcolm, but none of this wing's heavily sedated patients were going anywhere anytime soon. And even if they were, there were still other guards Malcolm could call in, should the kid have bailed again.

The doctor sighed, and then began his rounds.

To identify them, the John Does were numbered one through three. JD1, whom Malcolm checked first, had suffered a fracture that would likely inhibit his ability to move below the waist for some time. He had also suffered significant damage to his pancreas, along with a broken right hand, both of which would require surgery if they were ever given the go-ahead. But if something wasn't done soon, the man wouldn't last much longer.

Next was JD2, who had the worst injuries, suffering from a shattered pelvis and a fractured spine. It was certain that the man would never walk again, but given the amount of internal damage he had, it was unlikely the man would live through tomorrow.

He then headed for JD3, who looked to have taken the least damage: Only a single fractured column near the tail bone and a broken left leg they'd already splinted. The injuries were severe, but nothing compared to those of his companions. He would be able to walk again, but not without physical therapy.

As he approached JD3's room, Dr. Malcolm considered the men's appearances again. They appeared to be related, if not triplets: They all sported the same toned facial features and muscular body structure, along with dark blond hair and blue eyes. They resembled heavyweight champions or bodybuilders. But unlike most people in those groups, there was strong evidence of a dangerous amount of steroids in their blood. Along with traces of something else the lab had yet to identify.

None of them had woken up, last he checked, and Dr. Malcolm didn't expect them to. He had heavily drugged them to keep them in check until the FBI could investigate.

But when he opened the door, Malcolm dropped his clipboard. He stared at the bloody form under the covers, fearing something had gone horribly wrong. Had the drugs reacted badly to the unknown substance? He ran to the bed and threw off the sheet.

The body of the guard stared back at him, his outfit being the only thing that gave him away. The face Malcolm had come to know in passing was gone; his head looked as if it had imploded. The skull cavity was little more than a stew of brain matter and stagnant blood, the whites of the kid's eyes just barely discernible.

Suddenly, two hands slammed against either side of the doctor's head from behind him. He tried to scream, but nothing escaped. Everything went red, then black.

11

Wednesday, July 24ᵗʰ
Greenland Compound
7:27 AM (Greenland Time)

THE DARK ROOM OF THE LARGE MANSION WAS SPARSELY ADORNED BY THE COBWEBS OF LONG DEAD SPIDERS. The only illumination came from the large set of monitors before the lone occupant, who concentrated on them intently.

They displayed security footage from multiple systems, many from within the home itself, the man's paranoia of forces both domestic and cosmic deeming the extra security necessary. The rest were from systems he had hacked into, places he needed to see for his business, and some he wanted to see for personal reasons.

When one of the far monitors came to life, the owner shifted his unblinking eyes to the bright screen.

"Father, do you hear me?" asked a voice through one of the monitors.

There was no change in his demeanor as his son's voice echoed throughout the room. While he was pleased that his son had made it through the unforeseen trials, there was never time to be heartfelt.

"I read you, David," the owner replied in a scratchy, low voice. "Is the line secure?"

"Unclear. I had to use our doctor's cellphone," his son said.

The man at the computer worked to make sure the line was not being recorded before telling his son to proceed with caution. They couldn't be too careful.

"Our first attempt failed. We're all injured."

"Details."

"My left leg is broken. According to the doctor's charts, Evans has a broken hand and injured pancreas, and Erickson is immobile. As far as I know, I'm the first one of us up."

"I meant about the operation," his father growled. "What happened?"

"Erickson engaged early. He saw the target and went for it without consulting me." The shame in David's voice was obvious. *"With your permission, I would like to secure the others and be extracted."*

"Secure Evans. Leave Erickson."

Silence filled the line.

"You want us to just leave him here?" David finally said.

His father sighed. "He'll only hinder you, now."

"But he's my brother."

"And you're my son. I don't want to lose any more of you than I have to."

He knew his words would reverberate in David's head, and he hoped he wouldn't sense their true meaning. All three of them were his sons, and somewhere deep in his bruised and battered heart, he loved them. But this...

this was far more important than the bond of blood.

"We're taking him with us. I'm saving him."

The words carried the weight of a boy trying to be a man, frail and backed with false confidence. His father sighed, knowing it was a battle already lost.

"I can't stop you, can I?" he asked.

"Guess not."

His father let out a long, low groan. "Fine. Do what you can."

"Thank you," David said. *"Now, how do we get out of here?"*

"I'll see what I can do." His father lost himself for a moment, trying to decide if he needed to address the next stage of their plan.

Could they succeed without Erickson? Erickson's loss would mean a dramatic decline in available brute force, a lack that could endanger the mission. While David was the leader, he was not their strength. Erickson had the most muscle and was the most aggressive of the three. As long as the target went down, that was all he cared about. But not David. He'd probably waited, maybe even been too soft. Odds were, Erickson had acted accordingly after David had been too resistant. David was little more than a wannabe programmer with muscles and a gun, and he had the nerve to say that Erickson had stepped out of line?

While furious, their father tried to look at the failure in a positive light. It was still a victory, however minor. Benedict had to be scared, confused, and fearing for his investigators. They had accomplished that much, anyway.

"Where is the doctor?" he asked, hoping for the possibility of a hostage.

"He has since... retired from practice."

Undeterred, his father laid out the plan. "There's a chopper on the helipad now. It appears to be unguarded. If you can't land it somewhere safe, there should be two parachutes onboard." As he spoke, he was already typing away. "I'm in the hospital's security systems. I'll do what I can to make this easy for you."

12

DAVID (JD3) SPENT TWO TENSE MINUTES GATHERING HIS BROTHERS.

Evans (JD1) was still under light anesthesia when David woke him. After several frustrating attempts to bring him around, David retrieved a glass of water from the sink and splashed it over his brother's face, keeping a hand over his mouth to prevent any screams of surprise. As Evans got his bearings, they locked eyes, and David lowered his hand.

Evans didn't bother waiting for the plan. All he needed to know was that David had one, and to not deviate from it.

Together, they retrieved Erickson (JD2), placing him in a wheelchair before David led the charge into the quiet hallway.

On cue, the automatic doors slammed shut and locked themselves as the security system bent to their father's will. The hallways glowed red as sprinklers kicked on. The distractions helped the brothers escape, though they occasionally slipped on the wet tile floors.

The hallway before them was empty, a clear path to the helipad. David led the way, fighting to stay upright on his splinted leg while Evans pushed Erickson's wheelchair along, watching for any resistance.

They passed several rooms and hallways full of confused nurses who looked more interested in getting the doors to work than going after what they assumed were lost patients. It was fairly obvious that a glitch in the security system had accidentally activated a lockdown procedure.

The brothers were met with no challenge until they passed two guards who were trying desperately to open a pair of doors, a horde of drenched nurses looking on behind them. As the brothers passed by the windows, they saw realization in the guards' eyes.

They knew this was an escape attempt.

One officer retrieved his soaked radio and started shouting into it, his voice smothered by the chaos. But by then, the brothers had already burst through the next door, the flood of white light in the hallway the only sign of their departure.

Outside, as fire alarms continued to blare, David heard shouting and gunshots behind them. He almost wanted to laugh, as he knew they couldn't break through the security measures.

But as the doors of the helicopter parted, a crash from the hall proved him wrong. David watched a guard clumsily slide across the floor into view, then he noticed a second nearly fall into the hall as he tried not to lose his footing on the slippery floor. Before the pair could fire, the door to the roof slammed and locked itself, and the brothers hurried to the helicopter.

David and Evans lifted Erickson into the passenger's seat as guards made quick work of the last door. David ordered Evans to the copilot's seat as he got settled at the primary controls. David had flown a helicopter before, but he didn't have enough experience to feel confident in doing it again. He had to call upon every detail he could conjure from memory as the chopper slowly came to life.

The guards burst in as David managed to raise the helicopter off the ground. None of them opened fire, knowing the battle on their end was lost.

Once David knew what to do, he aimed the helicopter south, leaving the chaotic hospital far behind them.

Yet as the short flight went on, he knew that there was little hope of reaching their goal. The winds were pushing them north, fighting them as they neared the Santa Ana Mountains. He tried to correct his course, still hopeful to reach the Palm Desert before they had to ditch the helicopter.

In the darkness of the windy summer night, he couldn't hope to maneuver if he descended any further. They had to get out before they were forced down by the winds or the local authorities.

He ordered Evans to find the parachutes. His brother made it to the back, searching quickly through the many medical supplies, and eventually found two chutes. David carefully slipped one on before setting the helicopter to automatic pilot and climbing back with his brothers. As Evans slipped his on, David strapped Erickson's limp body to his own chute as best he could. The craft shook in the dry desert air, David already feeling the unintended loss of altitude. Once they were both ready, he opened the door.

They had been swept far north, beyond Irvine and into the foothills of the Santa Ana Mountains. Looking back through the cockpit, David saw what looked to be a cluster of lights in the foothills. Another town, he thought, and a small one. It was then that he knew exactly what to do.

He smiled, knowing there was still a chance of success as they jumped into the warm night.

13

THE NEXT MORNING, MICHAEL WOKE TO THE LOW HUM OF HIS AQUARIUMS' LIGHTS COMING ON. They were set on a timer that would mimic a day-and-night cycle, so before Michael even looked at his clock, he knew it was just after nine.

On any other day, he would have flown out of bed, dressed, and gotten ready for work. But the previous day was coming back to him, the requests from Benedict and his nurse to rest up and avoid stress. He felt compelled to defy them and go to work anyway, but he knew Benedict would be in town later.

Michael sighed. It was a battle already lost, but what was he going to say to Andrea? He felt bad for not calling her the night before. Now, he would have to drop the responsibility of running the shop on her again on incredibly short notice. It didn't feel right, but he didn't want Benedict to show up to an empty house, either.

Sitting up in bed, Michael could feel the bruising on his back. Resting his back against the headboard, he reached for his phone and dialed Andrea's cell.

"Hello?" came Andrea's kind voice after several rings, her Australian accent barely detectable after years spent in the States.

"Hey Ann, it's Michael. I'm sorry I didn't call you sooner, but Bene—"

"Benedict is coming, and you two need to talk with him," Andrea finished. "I heard. Aron called me last night."

He should have expected that. "Oh, okay. So, you're okay running the shop again?"

"You know I could run this place in my sleep."

It was true; she cared about the shop just as much as Michael did. As another one of Benedict's private investigators, she needed a day-to-day cover job to maintain appearances. While she occasionally worked as a make-up artist for large-scale movie and television productions, she still needed something that appeared to pay the bills. Benedict had introduced them all soon after Michael and Aron had joined DenCom, and they'd hit it off immediately. Her help was invaluable, especially when he and Aron were dragged away by work, and he reminded her of that before they ended the call.

"Not a problem," she said. "I just wish you could drop Granger off. We're in need of some quality girl time."

"Well, as soon as Fish and Wildlife gets off my ass, I'll bring her right over."

"In that case, I'll sic Benedict on them," she declared, which Michael thought she might actually do, given how much she loved the animal. "Later."

"Later. Call me if anything happens."

"Same to you," Andrea added, and they hung up.

Michael set the phone down, not bothering to text Aron the news he already knew. He lay back on the bed, letting the cool sheets dull the pain. His body relaxed, and before he knew it, he had fallen back asleep.

14

THE *BLUESTREAM*, A MODIFIED BOMBARDIER GLOBAL 6000, HAD JUST BEGUN ITS FINAL DESCENT INTO PALM SPRINGS. Benedict was already dreading the scorching temperatures as he watched the town grow closer.

Most people would have ditched their long coats in favor of t-shirts and shorts, but not Benedict. Admittedly, the idea of keeping the coat on at all times was ridiculous and childish, but he didn't care. And when it came to those few people he did see on a daily basis, he paid them enough not to care as well. Besides, what did they know? They had never needed to use one for shelter, as a tool, or to fight off a damned bear. When he had been lost in the Sierras, it had also been his security blanket, and he was not ashamed to admit it. Everyone had their own security items, whether they admitted it or not. Benedict's just happened to be a black wool coat that reached down to his calves.

But that didn't change the fact that it was going to make him sweat more than a hooker in church once they were on the ground.

What made him sweat now, though, was the fact that the three terrorists had escaped from the hospital. No one had thought it possible, given the severity of their injuries and the drugs they'd been given. They should have been out for hours, even days. How they'd managed to beat the drugs was still under investigation, although Benedict had his own theories.

From what they had gathered, the suspect referred to in reports as JD3 was the first to wake. From there, he woke JD1, and together, they'd retrieved their unconscious teammate. Then, some kind of virus or override program was uploaded to the security system, allowing them nearly unopposed passage to the hospital's helipad. The attackers piled into the helicopter and tried to escape to the southeast, but within ten minutes of takeoff, the aircraft had crashed into the Santa Ana Mountains just outside of Silverado. It was unclear if the crash was due to pilot error or inclement weather, but either way, the helicopter was now a burning wreck in the mountains northwest of Irvine.

Law enforcement and the fire department had been on the scene since early that morning, but they had yet to get close enough to the wreckage to find or secure any remains. In the California heat, the dry brush and trees had caught fire instantly, which led to what the authorities considered a bigger problem: A raging forest fire.

For the time being, the terrorists were a minor concern, the fire being a much more prominent threat to the historic town of Silverado, along with Irvine not far away. The terrorists surviving such a violent crash was all but impossible. So, for most people, the case was considered closed. Still, they wouldn't confirm it until the fires died down and they could reach the wreck.

For the moment, the media had no information except that a helicopter had crashed, and a fire had begun to spread down the mountainside. Silverado had been evacuated and Irvine placed under warning, so between the two, the news networks had their hands full. Linking the fire to the Spectrum attack would have been too much for the moment.

Although the area wasn't in a panic, the massive black pillar of smoke was an ominous presence over the surrounding cities, one that Benedict could easily see from his vantage point in the air. While he wanted to be there, to see the bodies himself, he had no doubt they were trapped in the smoldering wreckage. Reluctantly, Benedict allowed himself to relax.

As the *Bluestream* neared his destination, Benedict booked himself a room and planned on at least a one-night stay, perhaps longer if Michael and Aron weren't receptive to his ideas. The threat was most likely over, but even if they were wrong about that, he needed to convince them so or risk them panicking, or even leaving the company. While the repercussions would be felt for a while—and perhaps the consequences too—no one but Benedict needed to know them yet. At this point, it didn't matter who the terrorists were or where they were going.

No, Michael and Aron needed to be handled carefully.

He needed to ease them into the more probable truth gently, slowly. Besides, this could all be coincidence, and it could be irrelevant to the bigger picture.

To him, the alternative was not an option.

15

THAT NIGHT, DAVID, EVANS, AND A STILL DRUGGED ERICKSON PULLED INTO A CHEAP MOTEL OUTSIDE OF PALM SPRINGS, THE KIND WHERE QUESTIONS WOULDN'T BE ASKED.

After they ditched the helicopter, they landed half a mile from Silverado. As chaos erupted in the small town in the wake of the fire, they managed to find and steal a Jeep. With Erickson lying in the back, hidden by the fabric cover, they were able to drive out of town unopposed, merging with the traffic of evacuating residents.

The drive from Silverado to Palm Springs was made far longer than necessary by the crowded freeways. After leaving Irvine behind, the ride was smooth as they drove on to the former playground of the stars.

They arrived two hours before sunrise, checking in and parking their new Jeep out of the way so it wouldn't be seen. David and Evans carefully carried Erickson inside, placing him on the bed and allowing his body to settle.

Erickson was weak, and his brothers knew it. Every

time he was moved, they could hear the subtle clanking and shifting of his pelvis. They didn't discuss what to do for him; there was nothing more they could do. Erickson was strong, so if he had any chance of making it through the day, he would need to do it on his own.

Still, the brothers prepared themselves for the worst. As the early morning sun rose, David took the first watch, and Evans slept in the second bed. He hoped they wouldn't be confronted again, but even more so, he hoped Erickson's steady breathing wouldn't cease.

After he was sure Evans had fallen asleep, David reached for the rooms phone. He had to update their father on the situation, namely that they were where they needed to be. Their father had told them to ditch the chopper over the Palm Desert and find a way into town, but since that had not gone according to plan, he had no way of knowing they were still alive. If he was watching the news, he could have already thought they were dead. David cursed himself for waiting as long as he did as he dialed the number.

"Benedict is in Palm Springs," came their father's voice over the phone without a trace of concern or anger. Had he heard about the crash, or had he just assumed the plan had worked when he saw the Palm Springs area code? David knew it didn't matter. "He's your new target. Take him alive. If the other two get in the way, waste no time disposing of them."

"We have no weapons."

"I will arrange a delivery. I should be able to convince

a sympathizer to the cause to drop some off. Just be careful of a setup."

"All right, then what?"

His father typed away, then came back with an answer. "After you have your supplies, go to the Saguaro Hotel where Benedict is staying. If you can, apprehend him in the night. You can do preliminary reconnaissance in the area today." There was a pause. "How's Erickson doing?"

"He's close to gone," David said. He heard his father give a forced sigh.

"I'll see if I can include some medical supplies in the delivery to keep him asleep for a while. Once this is over, he will be cared for if he's..." he trailed off, then ended the conversation with one final, harsh note. "Remember, alive."

And the line went dead.

16

Wednesday, July 24th
Ramon Estados Condo Complex
Palm Springs, California
12:35 PM

GRANGER'S PURRING OUTSIDE MICHAEL'S DOOR WOKE HIM FOR THE SECOND TIME THAT DAY.

With a slow stretch and yawn, Michael got up and retrieved his clothes from the dresser across from him. He gently slipped the new clothes on, his shirt being the most difficult to manage with the still aching wound in his shoulder.

His room was adorned with a multitude of hanging artwork and ancient weaponry. Most of it was Egyptian in origin, or the work of local artists Michael had come to know. The majority of the art was original, some pieces commissioned to immortalize a lesson or memory. Some were from vacations, as exemplified by a large portrait of the view he had had from a beach house on Maui. Others were from dreams he remembered, like the small portrait of a silhouetted cowboy holding a sword against a gold background. His collection also included a Megalodon shark tooth, a pair of genuine samurai swords, a pair of bull's horns over the door, and much more. It was an impressive display that Michael still couldn't believe was his own.

But the centerpiece was a seventy-gallon reef aquarium he had established three years ago. It was home to a small colony of Garden Eels, a pair of Black Percula clownfish, and a Hawaiian Black Tang, among other high-end fish and corals.

Michael casually observed the tank as he forced himself through the pain. As always, the tank provided a calm, tranquil atmosphere that, for the moment, distracted him from his discomfort. The only other thing in life that had the ability to do so was Granger, who would always take the opportunity to fall asleep at his side.

But at the moment, she wasn't so calming. He saw her shadow pacing under the door, purring and meowing as she did so. Normally, she wouldn't be so forceful to see him, especially when he was still in his room, off limits to her.

She was telling him that something important needed his attention—or, at least, something *she* deemed important. But what?

With a chime of the doorbell, he got his answer.

He opened the door, Granger easily avoiding the quick motion as he did, and shouted that he would be out in a minute, not bothering to wait for a response before rushing to get presentable.

Moments later, he finished slipping on his shoes and headed for the door. As he entered the hallway, Granger greeted him eagerly.

The first few steps were unpleasant, but he began to feel better with every stride. He didn't know if he was actually getting better or getting used to the pain, but he took what he could get.

Michael shouted a greeting through the door, but there was no reply.

Something wasn't quite right.

Granger meowed to her master from the hall, almost encouraging him to let the unexpected guest in. Having no peephole to look through, Michael could do nothing but place his trust in the animal.

He unbolted the lock, leaving the chain on, just in case. He cracked open the door and nearly slammed it shut when he saw what was sitting on the landing.

There, in all its glory, was Aron's prize from Dave and Buster's: The stuffed dragon.

As he stared, unsure of the sight before him, the dragon gently fell over in the breeze and let out a roar from its voice box.

But over the roar, Michael could hear the whisper that told him all he needed to know:

"Damn it all to hell."

"Wow," Michael said. "I didn't know Smaug was such a potty mouth."

"Oh, bite me."

Michael undid the latch, and Benedict came into view as he reached for the monster, sporting his black coat and pendant as always. "I thought Aron would want this back, so I had my guys pick it up before I headed out," he explained.

Michael showed Benedict inside, where Granger strutted over to see him. He and Granger got along famously, which explained her calm behavior earlier. She probably knew it was him all along.

As Benedict reached down to pet her, Michael told him to make himself at home while he got Aron. Benedict protested, not wanting to disturb Aron if he wasn't ready, but Michael knew his roommate wouldn't want to be left out.

After one knock, Aron answered, telling Michael to come in. He was laid out on his African-style bedsheets in checkered bottoms and a white tank top. He sat up as Michael entered, placing a recently drained can of Red Bull among others in his trash can. His room was covered in posters for European gothic metal bands with names like Sirenia, Tristania, Within Temptation, and more than a few other groups with names Michael couldn't hope to pronounce. Other than that, the room was sparse. A concert recording played on the wall-mounted TV, suspended above a dresser where a lone jewelry box gathered dust.

"Look alive," Michael said. "Benedict just got in."

Aron bolted up. "I'll be ready in five," he said, and Michael left him to dress.

He came back to find Granger sprawled across Benedict's lap, the man petting her softly on the head as he looked around. The living room was sparsely decorated, the majority of the décor reserved for Michael's and Aron's rooms. The main walkway from the door went along the back wall of the living room, then led to the open dining room and adjacent kitchen.

Three aquariums dotted the room: A freshwater Cichlid tank sat opposite an L-shaped couch where Benedict sat, and two saltwater tanks were affixed to the wall to his right. While the saltwater aquariums were coral tanks similar to the one in Michael's room, the Cichlid tank was the main showpiece. It was a ninety-gallon tank filled with neon-colored fish, mostly from Africa's Lake Tanganyika, a large painting of which hung above the tank.

Michael had pulled a lot of strings to get the aquariums approved by the landlord, who wasn't easily swayed about pets but was easily swayed by money. Michael was considering buying the complex at some point so he could make the condo beneath his part of the home as well, the bottom level reserved for the large aquariums of his dreams.

Hanging in the middle of the room was an out-of-style gold chandelier. It didn't match the rest of the room, but Michael liked it too much to let it go. On the far wall, a large flatscreen TV was mounted above a pair of sliding glass doors that led to the patio. The rest of the house was sparsely decorated, save for a few scattered paintings and pictures.

Stepping down onto the lower floor of the living room, Michael took a seat on the end of the couch just to the right of Benedict and Granger.

"So, any updates or news? Do we know who the attackers were?" he asked.

"Yeah, there is some news, but it better wait until Aron gets here. It's kind of a long story," Benedict said. He then proceeded to give Michael some bullet points, anyway: "But as far as I.D.'s go, we still have zip. No fingerprints matched, no wallets or credit cards on them. Just some cash that was traced, but I'll get to that later. The only other thing we got from them was some blood that showed a lot of NS and steroids."

"NS?" Michael asked.

"Nerve Suppressors," Benedict clarified. "They cause a sizable drop in pain receptor sensitivity. A guy could get shot and walk it off with this stuff."

"Never heard of it."

"That's because it's not public. At least, this type isn't. Similar medications are used for arthritis, but this stuff was created by a fitness company a couple years ago that I heard about... through channels. They were hoping to market it to people who wanted to work out harder and longer, but the risk of someone working themselves to death was obvious. At the request of some friends of mine in the government, I bought the company and shut it down. I thought I had everything they made destroyed, but it looks like they got ahold of the same medication. Along with the steroids, it was unlikely they even noticed the extent of their injuries."

"Great," Aron said from the hallway, having caught the

tail end of the statement. "So now what?"

Michael looked over at Benedict as Aron had a seat beside him.

"Well, I guess I should deliver the bad news first, if you don't mind me being blunt."

They nodded.

He sighed. "The three men broke out of the hospital early this morning via helicopter."

Michael felt his jaw drop. Benedict went over the timeline and what they knew. Once he reached the point where the chopper crashed, Aron cut in.

"That's what crashed by Silverado?"

Benedict nodded, before filling Michael in. "It crashed when they tried to make a course correction, or so I've been told. The crash caused a forest fire that's made it nearly impossible to find remains, but I doubt they'll find much."

Michael sat back, stunned. Aron looked down at the floor. Even Granger sensed the tension and stopped begging for attention.

"Where do you think they were heading?" Aron asked, not bothering to look up.

"East. As for a specific destination, we don't have any hard evidence to support that they even had one," Benedict replied.

Michael's eyes widened.

"Here," he said quietly, then locked his gaze on Benedict. "They were coming here, weren't they?"

17

"MICHAEL, WHAT ARE YOU–?" ARON STARTED, BEFORE MICHAEL INTERRUPTED.

"They could have been coming for us. We're right in their flight path!"

"So's Perris, Hemet, Cabazon, and about a dozen other small desert towns," Benedict protested. "And beyond that, they could have been heading for the Mojave. Maybe they planned to land there at night, out of sight of the police, so they could move on to a hideout. Hell, for all we know, they may have wanted to try for Mexico!"

Benedict could be right. While Palm Springs could have been their goal, it was one of literally dozens of other towns in their possible flight path. And, as Benedict had already pointed out, they could have been planning to ditch the helicopter in the desert. Michael sat back, taking the idea in and wondering if he had just been jumping at shadows.

"We don't know for sure that they died, do we?" Aron asked.

"There's nothing that says they made it out, but law enforcement won't write them off until they have bodies. We know the helicopter had two parachutes on board, but it's unlikely they were able to escape in their condition. Plus, if the burn area is any indication, they may have been too close to the ground for the parachutes to do them any good."

"If they weren't in any condition to escape the helicopter, how the hell were they able to get out of the hospital in the first place?" Michael pointed out.

Benedict shook his head. "Who knows? But at this point, I think it's safe to let it go."

"*What*?" was Michael's first response, a hint of disgust grazing the word.

"You really think we need to just *forget* about this? How can we let this go?" Aron asked, giving Michael's own thoughts voice.

Benedict's tone grew defensive. "Because there's no solid evidence that they wanted *you* in particular. You were caught in the crossfire of a terrorist attack, and thank God you both survived!"

"But they chased me down and put a gun to my head! You think that's coincidental?" Michael asked.

"You told me that you panicked, remember? In that panic you ran, you made yourself a target, and you were the last one there left alive when the rest of the crowds cleared out."

"I'm sorry, I can't accept that, Benedict."

"Then accept this: They're dead. One of them was nearly dead when they left the hospital, and one of them would've be gone within the month if he didn't get help. That leaves the third with a broken leg, an injured spine and two deadweights to lug around. Do you really think they would've made it out of that helicopter alive?"

"But shouldn't we be worried that there's more of

them out there?"

Benedict threw up his hands. "Who the hell would want *you*? If they had a problem with your work, don't you think they would try to off *me* first?"

Michael was left without a comeback. Benedict's logic was sound, but it wasn't enough to convince him that this was the end of it. He watched as Benedict sank back in the couch, letting himself calm down.

Things had escalated too quickly.

Moments of silence passed before Benedict continued. "Either way, I don't think we have to worry about them anymore. It's not likely that they'll have any support in the country."

"Meaning?" Aron asked.

"Michael, remember when I told you about the bills we traced?"

Michael nodded.

Benedict sat back up. "We traced them to an exchange kiosk at Stockholm International airport. About a week ago, they exchanged roughly 500 Swedish Krona for American bills. We're still waiting for an exact match of who the bills were given to so we can find them and their flight, but from what we gathered so far, it was only the three of them. They traveled light and alone. They probably bought the guns once they made it into the country."

"But why us? Why the Spectrum?" Michael asked.

"Because you were good targets in a packed shopping center. I shouldn't have to explain the rest," Benedict replied.

"So, it was just wrong place, wrong time?"

"As far as you being there, yes. The attack itself had to have been planned out months in advance. There are plenty of terrorist organizations who could be responsible, and I'm sure they'll be pretty loud about it when they decide to claim the honor of killing nearly two dozen infidels in a decadent American mall."

Michael only stared at Benedict as he sat back, resting his case.

"That's it, then?" Michael asked as Granger resumed her begging.

"That's the reality. I, for one, am happy you both got out okay, and I'm going to do all I can to find out who did this."

Michael didn't want to admit it, but he was beaten. He had no comeback, no rebuttal. While the explanation didn't make him feel any better, it made sense. It wasn't an attack on DenCom, not on himself or Aron. It was a tragic event he would never forget, but it wasn't going to help anything if he kept worrying over it. He and Aron weren't the reason those people had died. It was time to let it go, to move on.

As if on cue, Benedict broke the silence.

"So, lunch, anyone?"

18

THE THREE MEN LEFT MICHAEL'S CONDO SHORTLY AFTER THEIR CONVERSATION ENDED. They piled into the Rolls-Royce, the driver from the previous day at the wheel. Benedict sat up front while Michael and Aron shared the back.

The day before them was a simple one. First, they would stop in at Modern Aquaria so Benedict could see Andrea and check in on the shop. Then, they would drive to The Saguaro Hotel, where Benedict was staying, for dinner at the hotel restaurant. From there, they would go their separate ways, Benedict leaving for Denver the following day.

Modern Aquaria's new location was hard to miss when driving down Palm Canyon Drive. Roughly the size of a small grocery store, it was the largest aquarium shop within a fifty-mile radius. The neon sign, bright in luminosity and color, caught the eyes of everyone on the street. People often came in and out with jugs of saltwater and other supplies, always creating activity in front of the shop. Being the only supplier of what was considered a luxury hobby in a luxury town, they almost always had business. At this point, even without DenCom, Michael could live like a king off the place if he chose to.

The driver pulled up to the curb, let his three passengers out, then returned to the car as they entered the shop.

As always, Benedict let out an audible gasp as they walked in and he saw the main attraction: The massive shark tank. The sight, on the rare occasion he would visit, always left him speechless.

The large, circular tank was what brought many people to the store from the street. Extending nearly ten feet around and seven feet tall, the tank was sparsely decorated with seaweed stalks and a rocky core where the filtration intakes and outflows were hidden. Circling the tank were a pair of leopard sharks that stayed relatively near each other, along with several other fish that always made way for the four-foot-long sharks.

Behind it were seven rows of aquariums: Three devoted to saltwater fish and corals, and four reserved for tropical freshwater stock. The rest of the store was dedicated to supplies, including a pair of large water containers that housed the pre-mixed saltwater sold to hobbyists. The shop was nearly three times the size of the old location where Benedict had first found Michael, and was infinitely more professional-looking.

"Hey, stranger," came Andrea's light Australian accent from behind the counter to their left. She hurried over to Benedict, hugging him as she did all her friends. Benedict returned the hug, all the while stealing glances around the store he co-owned with Michael yet never had much of a chance to see. "What are you all doing here? I thought you guys had a meeting," she said as they let each other go.

"It didn't take as long as we thought, so I figured I would drag Michael and Aron around with me before I fly off tomorrow," Benedict said.

Andrea smiled, but gave Michael and Aron a questionable glance—more in a sarcastic way than anything else—but they could tell she was concerned.

"Don't go getting mad at them. This was all me. They didn't know we'd be going out until I showed up," Benedict informed her.

Andrea let a grin appear on her face. "All right, I guess I can't stay mad at you," she said to Michael in particular as she stepped forward and gave him a small, welcoming hug.

"Now, if you'll excuse me, I think I'm gonna take a look around, get sad that I can't take any fish friends home, and then get some ice cream to make me feel better," Benedict joked.

"It's tradition, I suppose," Andrea said, then shooed him on his way. After he was out of earshot, she changed the subject. "So how'd that go?"

"Not great," Michael said. "I got into an argument with him this morning over the Spectrum."

Andrea was shocked. "That's not like you guys. You're normally on the same page."

"I know. It's just hard for me to shake the idea that

they weren't after us."

"Why would they want you? I mean, all I saw on the news was that some random guys shot up the mall and Aron took them out. You think they were after you?"

Michael filled her in on the whole story, along with what Benedict said had happened to the suspects early that morning. She took a long, hard look at both men, searching for any telltale signs of exaggeration. It was obvious she saw none.

"All we do is look into mysteries and conspiracies, like if Walt Disney's head is hidden in one of the parks. It's nothing valuable to anyone other than Benedict, if it's even valuable at all," Andrea said.

"That's what I thought, too," Michael replied, "but there are a lot of crazies on DenCom's tail. I guess I was worried that Benedict underestimated them."

"I can agree there," Aron said. "I'm sure some of them would be willing to act, since being dead would kind of put a damper on the whole 'discover the world's secrets' thing."

"You don't sound convinced," Andrea said, turning to Michael.

"I'm convinced," Michael insisted, this time with more lightness in his voice. But he wasn't convincing anyone, not even himself.

Andrea could only smile. "Well, anyway, I'm glad you guys are safe. So, you're going to be out for a while?"

"Just to lunch, I think. Maybe a few hours, at most," Michael replied.

"I wouldn't be surprised if Benedict wanted to drag us all around town and make a day out of it, though," Aron added.

It wasn't uncommon; it was clear that Benedict was lonely, and he obviously wanted the company, so Michael and Aron had never had the heart to tell him no if and when he asked. They both agreed that even though Benedict had been an acquired taste at first, after years of working together, he may as well have been another one of their friends, and they wanted to treat him as such. Benedict, of course, had never objected; whenever he was in town, he'd drag them to shows, a local club or wherever he felt like having fun that night. Where they'd go from the Saguaro was anyone's guess.

"All right, well, if you guys need me to come and break the tension or whatever, my shift ends in two hours. Don't hesitate to text me."

Michael smiled. "Andrea, you know I could let you off a little early, if you want to have lunch with us."

"Oh, no, I want to stay if you don't need me. The neon dottybacks are ready to start laying, so if I can, I want to see it."

Michael couldn't blame her. They'd been trying to breed their own stock as a pet project for months, and things were finally looking up.

Michael wished he could have stayed as well, but then, he caught a glimpse of Benedict heading toward them and knew it was time to head out. After a long goodbye, Michael and Aron rejoined Benedict in the Rolls-

Royce.

19

"EARTH TO ARON. Repeat, Earth to Aron. Come in, Aron," Benedict said with his hand over his mouth, imitating radio chatter. "Your steak is here. Repeat, your steak is here. If you wish for Benny-Boo to eat it, please say nothing."

"Benny-Boo?" Aron asked, snapping back to reality after hearing Benedict's old pet name. He looked down at his glass. "What the hell are we drinking?"

They shared a laugh as the waitress set their food down on the table.

After leaving Michael's shop, the three men found themselves having a late lunch. Benedict had called ahead to see if he needed to reserve a table, but was surprised to find that the restaurant was nearly empty. Two or three other small parties were spread out, allowing them to converse in relative privacy. As they ate in silence, Michael noticed that Aron was drifting away again. This was a common occurrence for him, to simply slip out of the world around him and into his own head.

"You think he's flashing back to his old flying days?" Benedict asked as he took a bite of his steak.

This caught Aron's attention. "Sure, I would just *love* to go back to flying slapped-together pieces of garbage over LA again. Yeah, those were the good days!"

"So you're still glad I offered you the job at the shop?" Michael asked.

"Trust me, I'm enjoying myself," Aron said. "I was an awful pilot who was lucky enough to know how to take off and land. Not to mention it was hard to keep the banners straight enough for people to read about some C-grade lawyer."

"Good to hear. So, you won't mind being on vacuum duty the rest of the week?" Michael asked, and they shared another laugh as Aron smiled, rolling his eyes.

Half an hour later, they were done with their meals and ready to leave. It was three in the afternoon, and it looked as if they would beat the traffic home. But as Aron had predicted, Benedict began talking about his plans for later that night.

"I was thinking of taking the Skyway tram up the mountain for a while," he said. "I used to do it with my parents at this little place in the Rockies, but I've never gone on the Palm Springs one before, so I thought I would give it a shot while I was in town." He followed his words with the inevitable: "You guys want to come along?"

Michael and Aron couldn't help glancing at each other. Although Benedict had asked, right on cue, to extend their outing, it wasn't like him to prefer one of the more touristy attractions to the local scene. Not to mention that out of everything Palm Springs had to offer, the tram would have been the last thing on either man's mind.

A short distance out of town, the aerial tram carried people up Mt. San Jacinto. The often-snow-capped peak loomed over Palm Springs, its foothills grazed by the outer suburbs. Mt. San Jacinto boasted the best view for miles, looking out over the desert cities and on to the Imperial Valley and Salton Sea. It was a quaint attraction that Michael hadn't bothered with since he first moved to town.

He thought over the offer. It was a choice between relaxing at home with Granger and extending their rare outing, the latter possibly mending some still tender feelings in the process. Even though the meal had been a good one, the residuals of their earlier argument had managed to dampen the joviality, an unspoken elephant in the room among the jokes and laughs. Michael didn't want to end Benedict's visit on a bad note, especially since Benedict clearly didn't want to, either.

While he couldn't help but feel tense after yesterday's events, Michael was starting to accept that he had overreacted. Benedict was right: There was no way the terrorists could have survived the crash. If they had survived and they were, in fact, after him, he'd already given them plenty of opportunities throughout the day to take him out. But they hadn't. No terrorists had tried to cut him down. No monster had jumped out from the shadows and yelled, "Boo!"

Besides, getting out of the desert and into the fresh mountain air might do him some good. Either way, the look on Aron's face was clear: He'd already made his mind up.

"I'm in, you?" Michael asked, and Aron didn't take long to answer.

"Sure, it's been a while. Could be fun."

With that, they threw their napkins down on the table and headed for the car.

20

THEIR DRIVER DROPPED THEM OFF AT THE VALLEY TRAM STATION, IF IT COULD EVEN BE CALLED THAT. It was more of a tourist trap than a station, a gift shop thinly disguised as a waiting area for the tram.

As Benedict wandered into the gift shop, Michael and Aron took friendly bets over how much money they thought their boss would spend, and how much stuff he would leave with. As the intercom signaled that it was their turn to ride, to their surprise, Benedict returned to them with open hands and a promise that he would return when the day was over. For the moment, both Michael and Aron had lost their bets.

Since they were among the first on the tram, the three of them promptly claimed a section in the front as the rest of the passengers were herded in like cattle behind them. Soon, the large, circular car started up the mountain, slowly rotating as it ascended Mt. San Jacinto, allowing everyone a 360-degree view of the mountain and surrounding desert scenery.

The ride was smooth, except for the crossing of the support towers, which caused the car to sway and the majority of the occupants to give an excited but unnecessary shout.

Between this, the constant spinning, and a slight case of claustrophobia setting in, Michael started to feel sick. Although the ride was still enjoyable, he was planning on taking it easy once they reached the peak. Over the course of the day, most of the pain had diminished significantly, but every few steps, he'd have to slightly adjust his arm to relieve some minor aching. It was more an annoyance than anything, but the feeling of being in a giant, spinning can of sardines was not helping.

The car came to a gentle, swaying stop as it reached the station at the mountain's peak. Everyone filed out and began to explore the top of the mountain, a bombardment of camera flashes celebrating their arrival.

Once they were inside the station, Michael, Aron, and Benedict split up; Benedict went to walk the mountain path, Aron headed for the museum, and Michael walked upstairs to the small café, where he got a lemonade to calm his stomach and nerves. The air outside was typically forty degrees cooler than the desert below, and he hadn't had a chance to prepare for the sudden drop in temperature before agreeing to come along.

For once, during one of Benedict's visits to Palm Springs, bringing that black coat had actually been a good idea.

As Michael sat down at a two-person table on the

balcony, he watched his two friends wander off to their own business. Once they were out of sight, he found himself gazing out the wall of windows facing the peak. The sky was turning shades of orange and purple, illuminating the mountain in a beautiful display of colors that wouldn't last long.

Beyond the mountains, a small storm had kicked up. Although not typical this time of year, the rain would be a godsend to the parched landscape if it ever made it beyond the small range. Seeing this reminded Michael that summer was nearing its end, and storms would become more and more common as the months dragged on.

He wondered how many would come. He didn't want to set his expectations too low, or too high.

Michael nursed his lemonade like a fine liquor as he watched the clouds dance outside the lodge. They slid through the peaks and dipped down near the trees as they went by, coating the mountain in fleeting layers of fog. As the sunset faded into dusk, Michael thought the summit was being drenched in a haze of rain, but he couldn't be sure. He would get his answer if Benedict came back from his hike soaking wet.

As Michael lost himself in the view, he barely registered the familiar bulky figure in his periphery. For a split second, they locked eyes. His mind racing, Michael forced himself to stare at the stranger, but the man drifted out of sight down the spiral stairs, lost among the other tourists.

No, not here. It was impossible; it couldn't have been one of them. Must be a lookalike, he reasoned, paranoia attempting to reclaim him, tricking him.

But that gaze. The man had the same aggressive stare he'd seen on the murder darting behind the sunglass kiosk at the Spectrum.

His stomach plummeted. He knew that look couldn't lie.

21

SURROUNDED BY A SPARSE BUT NOTICEABLE HERD OF TOURISTS, BENEDICT WOUND DOWN THE MOUNTAIN PATH AND THROUGH THE FOREST, NOT FAR FROM DAVID'S LINE OF SIGHT.

Evans had already called in saying he'd spotted Ridding in the cafe and Sanderson heading into the museum.

Benedict was finally within their reach, although it hadn't been according to plan. If it *had* been, they would have killed Ridding back at the Spectrum and waited for Benedict to start his own investigation, as it was almost certain that Benedict would handle the murder of his best investigator personally. They would have waited for him to slip up, and his own inexperience in the field would be his downfall.

But they hadn't planned on Sanderson's little show of bravery. Or stupid luck.

Earlier that day, the brothers had received a small delivery from the handful of sympathizers in the States. It consisted of several firearms, assorted clothing, cell phones, and a few pieces of outdated medical equipment. After hooking Erickson up and redressing his wounds, David and Evans knew they needed to finish what they had started.

They'd passed the hotel several times, noting the Rolls-Royce outside as a possible giveaway that Benedict was still present. After three recon passes, they circled for a fourth when they caught a glimpse of Michael and Aron getting in the back seat. After trailing them out of town and to the station, David decided that they should follow Benedict and the others to the top of the mountain, where Benedict would be much easier to corner and trap. They'd let him get a head start, and, lo and behold, there he was. Unprotected, unprepared, almost begging to be caught.

They had never dreamed that Benedict would be this stupid. Sure, they knew he wasn't as experienced as he'd led people to believe, his agents often taking the brunt of what little action the company saw. But short of two trips to the mountains doing God only knew what, it was debatable if Benedict had even left his office in the past several years. The answer had been obvious when he started leaving a trail that any amateur could follow.

But securing him, that would be another matter.

They had started with the *Bluestream*. Their father had tried to hack into the advanced controls, take over, and send the plane their way with Benedict trapped inside. However, the program proved too volatile, likely ending with the crash of the aircraft and a digital trail that would have led right to them. And how would they get information from a burnt corpse?

Apprehending him on foot seemed to be the only logical way. Once Benedict was alone—or close to alone— they would take him and put him at gunpoint. After stealing a pair of motocross bikes from a nearby ranger cabin, they'd force Benedict onto the back of one of them, knocking him out or strapping him down if necessary. From there, their father had the plan all worked out. It was still a long shot, but it was still more likely to work than their old plan.

At least, David had thought so, until he saw Benedict answer a phone call and fall back from the rest of the group. Benedict tensed and grew agitated as he spoke on the phone, starting to look around before thinking better of it. With a grunt of frustration, Benedict slowly retraced his steps along the path, his pace quickening as he neared the station.

David reached for his gun, but he knew it wasn't worth it. Benedict was already too far away for a bullet to do much damage, let alone target accurately. Instead, he pulled out his cell phone as he trailed Benedict at a safe distance.

22

MICHAEL ENDED THE CALL AND LOOKED BACK AT THE STAIRS THAT HE'D WATCHED THE MAN DESCEND ONLY MINUTES AGO, FRUITLESSLY TRYING TO CALM HIMSELF. There was no way he could have been mistaken, and he knew they needed to get down the mountain as soon as possible.

Benedict had been abrupt in his reply. Michael could hear the subtle tinge of anger in his voice over the phone, but he couldn't intimidate Michael into changing his mind.

And, if he turned out to be wrong, getting chewed out by Benedict would be the lesser of two evils.

Michael sat up and started for the stairs, leaving his half-finished lemonade behind. He couldn't pick out the man in the crowd, but he did lock eyes with Aron, who was flipping through t-shirts in the gift shop. Once on the ground level, he gave a small wave to his friend, signaling him to come over with a forced smile that he knew Aron could see right through.

As they reached each other by the wall of windows, Benedict marched in, and Michael could already sense his annoyance.

"What's going on?" Aron asked.

"I think I saw one of them, the men from the Spectrum," Michael replied. "There could be more of them here."

"You *think* it was one of them?" Benedict asked.

"Positive."

Benedict swore under his breath. "Michael, there's a big difference between 'You think' and 'You're positive.' You're sure you're not jumping the gun?"

Michael felt his hands ball into fists. He wasn't sure whether or not the pun had been intended, and he didn't feel like asking. "Benedict, I know what I saw. We have to haul ass down the mountain before the Spectrum repeats itself. Do you want that kind of guilt on you?"

Benedict's eyes grew wide. Michael hoped he'd conveyed the certainty of his conviction, but he feared Benedict was about to tell him off.

"You're sure," Benedict said, barely audible to anyone else but Michael.

"You can scold me later if I'm wrong," Michael promised.

"Don't think I won't," Benedict warned, before adding, "We can head down and work out the rest later, but I was hoping I wouldn't have to use this."

He reached into his right pocket and produced what looked like a folded leather wallet, but the trained eye could spot what it was immediately. He flipped it open, and Michael and Aron's jaws dropped.

"FBI!" Aron nearly shouted.

"Where the hell did you get that?" Michael asked.

"A favor from the big man," Benedict explained. "He said to utilize it when dealing with any threats to us or national security. And if you're right, this fits into one or even both of those categories."

"So, you're FBI?" Aron asked.

"Well, yes and no, but that doesn't matter now. What matters is that it should be able to get us our own car, at the very least. If you're sure they're only after us, then no one else will be at risk," Benedict said, then moved swiftly toward the tram dock, closely followed by Michael and Aron.

Benedict approached the lone security guard and flashed his badge.

"FBI. We need to get down the mountain, a-sap, empty car," he said, using the most serious tone he could muster.

The guard looked over the badge, then looked skeptically at the three men. From his right side, he unclipped a device that looked like an oversized calculator and typed in the ID number on the badge. Michael feared that the number would prove to be false, sending them all to jail.

However, it proved to be legitimate.

"What's this about?" the guard asked, handing the flip case back.

"Sir, we don't have time to explain," Michael interrupted, trying to act the part, sans the black suit and sunglasses. He felt he had done well, but he could tell Benedict was irritated at Michael having stolen the limelight. Undeterred, Michael leaned closer so his next words wouldn't frighten anyone around them. "All you need to know is that the safety of everyone on this mountain is at risk. This needs to be done as quietly as possible so there's no panic."

The guard looked them all over again, still not convinced, but he eventually caved. "Fine. There's another car coming in a moment. But if this is a joke, I'll have your hides. Got it?"

The three of them nodded and he showed them past the long line, shouting a cover story that a priority descent was needed for a sick man. Most people looked at Michael, who was actually starting to feel sick the longer the wait became.

23

DAVID COULD HARDLY CONTAIN THE CASCADE OF OBSCENITIES STREAMING THROUGH HIS HEAD AS HE SURVEYED THE AREA.

Where the hell was Benedict? David had lost him for a minute after his target entered the lodge, but relied on Evan's vantage point inside to keep track of him.

He feverishly waited for the call, the assurance that Benedict wasn't onto them, but no such call came. He had sent the warning text to Evans only seconds ago, but already worried that it hadn't gotten through, that the signal on top of the mountain would keep them from each other.

For an eternal moment, David was left alone, panicking over the disappearance of their target, fearing they'd been spotted. If they had, there was no way of getting Benedict or his two investigators while still on the mountain. If Benedict was smart, he'd already be readying the *Bluestream* for takeoff at Palm Springs International.

If so, there wasn't a chance in Hell they'd catch Benedict anytime soon. Their father had ruled out a home abduction long before they'd left on the mission. It would be too risky to get past measure after measure of Benedict's home security, not to mention that of DenCom Tower.

And securing Michael or Aron at their own home? Still plausible if Benedict left them behind; worst case scenario, they'd make good hostages. However, there was little chance of them slipping up that badly again.

David reached for his cell phone, desperate for information. It was a mistake to deviate from the established plan, but he needed to know how things looked.

One ring came and went.

David's breathing gradually turned to hyperventilating.

Two rings.

He could feel his heart thumping like a bass drum. His right hand began to tremble.

Three rings.

He swore under his breath. Was he having a heart attack? No, that wasn't it. A panic attack?

Four rings.

His stomach contracted. He fought not to wretch as Evans answered.

"I can see them. They're all together. Benedict looks off. Michael's worse. I think they're talking about leaving."

David tried to gather himself. He was still breathing heavily, growing dizzy, resisting the urge to give in, to fall to the cold ground and let it pass. He wasn't thinking clearly. He didn't feel in the moment. The rest of the world was an anomalous blur to him now, but he kept fighting, kept trying to pull through.

"Are...? Are they...?" the words came out between heaving breaths.

"They're talking to a security guard now," Evans said.

No, no, no, no, no! David's mind raced. There wasn't much time. If they were going to try something, they needed to try it *now*.

"David, get in here. I think we can take them if we meet them at the car."

The words were far away, but David understood them. He took one careful step forward toward the lodge on the cement path, resting his splinted leg on the ground as firmly as possible before taking another.

"Damn it, they're heading for the car now. Hurry up!"

Only feet away, David forced himself to rush the stairs, toppling over as he reached the deck floor, the phone falling several feet away. People rushed to his aid, making sure the already-injured man was okay. He could feel them, grabbing him, pulling him up against his will, asking questions as he reached for his phone, pressing it to his ear.

"David, what do I do?"

At once, everyone let go of David.

One man, too slow to register the gun drawn from David's coat pocket, took a bullet to the ribs as the barrel was thrust into his side. He fell with a shout, and people fled.

Hobbling through the doors into the lodge, David lifted his gun once more, parting the sea of frightened tourists. Running as best he could on the splinted leg, he screamed his orders into the phone.

"Shoot the guard! Now!"

24

MICHAEL, ARON, AND BENEDICT PUSHED THROUGH THE HORDE OF CONCERNED AND ANGRY TOURISTS TO THE FRONT OF THE LINE WHERE THE NEXT SPINNING TRAM CAR WAS JUST BEGINNING TO PULL IN. As it did, the officer entered the tram car ahead of them, then quietly explained the real situation to the young woman driving, telling her to get them to the bottom of the mountain as soon as possible.

She nodded as he left, then called the station below as the three men took his place.

The car started down the mountain seconds later, and they all looked back just in time to see the officer's head explode and his body topple over the edge of the cliff.

The driver screamed as the car drifted farther away from the station. Michael tried to keep himself from vomiting as blood and brain matter splattered over the car, propelled outward by the force of the blast.

The killer—the one Michael had seen on the stairs—stepped out from the fleeing crowd, just behind where the guard had been. Soon, a second man stumbled in as the deck cleared, but as he did, the first man aimed the gun in his quivering right hand not at the tram car, but *above* it. This confused its unwitting occupants for a brief moment until the hobbling man screamed his order like a banshee.

"Stop the car! Stop it!"

Michael felt the pings of the bullets on the suspended

car's roof. Then, they all heard the sound of snapping from above, and on each side, a large, black line swung away from them as the car settled and more bullets flew.

Then, they stopped, as if the attackers saw something they didn't. Michael soon realized what had halted the attack:

The car's speed was increasing, slowly but steadily.

Michael looked at the rest of them as the car passed the first support tower, which rushed by far too fast.

It dawned on them all: The main pulley cable for the tram car had been severed. Now, nothing was stopping the tram from flying down the mountain; the only things keeping it aloft were the guidance cables on either side.

But those wouldn't slow it down. They would only guide it to an explosive end at the station below.

"Pull the emergency brake!" Aron shouted to the driver.

She already had her hands gripped tightly around the large red lever, pulling with all her strength. "It's not working!"

Aron ran back to help her, fighting gravity as he reached for the lever. The woman stepped back, hoping that Aron had the power to pull it and stop the car. But the brake still wouldn't budge.

Before Aron could try anything else, the car lurched back, then forward as it passed the second tower, the screeching of metal audible in the cabin as the tram cleared the slight hump and picked up speed again. Michael was thrown down, as were Benedict and the driver before their rapid descent continued. Silence followed, only broken by the roaring wind through the few open windows.

And Aron's screams.

Michael looked to see a bloody gash running from Aron's wrist to the crux of his left arm where the handle was buried in his flesh. Aron fell back, the still unyielding handle sliding free as he crashed onto the floor in agony. Benedict and the driver stumbled to his aid, Michael unable to get to his feet in time.

The third tower passed in a blur, meaning the fourth and final tower was only seconds away.

"Everyone get to the center of the car!" Michael shouted over the deafening roar.

He struggled to maintain his footing until they all came together, Benedict and the driver pulling Aron along. They clung to the center column and support bars, able to do little more than wait.

And hope.

The car hit the fourth tower hard, lurching at a nearly ninety-degree angle as the guides forced it up. Screeching and bending metal obscured their screams as the car came down again and continued on the final leg of its journey.

But they all felt it, the subtle swaying that became more prevalent as the car descended into the station. Left, right, left, right, higher and higher each time like a crazed, manic pendulum as they realized with horror that they were going to be crashing into the station at an angle.

They held on for their lives as the car crashed through the main lobby, snapping free of its metal supports. Powered only by its own momentum, it rolled on its side through the evacuated lobby and crashed through the other windowed side.

Soaring through the air, it came to a rolling crash on the main road that led up to the station. Gathering even more speed as it rolled down the mountainside, it narrowly avoided evacuating tourists and swerving cars that did their best to clear a path.

It only began losing momentum as it grazed the trees and rocks along the side of the road. After a full minute of rolling, the battered, beaten tram car strayed into the soft desert sands, where it landed upside down with one final metallic cough.

Above them, storm clouds gathered, and the subtle roar of helicopter rotors was smothered by the deafening clap of distant thunder.

25

ANDREA STEPPED CLUMSILY INTO HER APARTMENT, PLACING HER JACKET AND OSTRICH LEATHER PURSE ON THE PREDATOR STATUE BEFORE COLLAPSING ONTO THE COUCH.

She'd finished her shift at the shop, not bothering to stay when there were no signs the dottybacks would be laying today. After texting Michael, she knew she wouldn't be interested in joining them. He said they were heading up the mountain, and that they wouldn't be back until later that night. She had declined the offer to meet them at the station, but hoped they had a good time.

Andrea looked around in an exhausted daze, studying her movie memorabilia and trying to decide how she wanted to relax that night. The living room looked like a film museum; busts and famous movie props—most were replicas, but some were originals—sat on glass shelves scattered around the room. There was also a life-sized Batman statue, more than a few alien swords and daggers mounted on the wall behind her, and a statue of the original Predator she used as a coatrack, since the old thing was falling apart, anyway.

It was a nerd's dream. Her dream. The only thing missing was the one thing she desperately longed for: A pet.

Andrea had never owned an animal in her adult life, fearing her hectic Hollywood schedule and responsibilities would lead to unintentional neglect. Still, she had always longed for some kind of companionship in the house, since she could only talk to Batman or the Predator for so long.

Regardless, she did live happily. Benedict had advised her not to live too lavishly and draw attention to herself, if at all possible. If she had to guess, most of the other investigators had probably put their money away for retirement, or at least until they could afford to move away from prying eyes. She understood that approach, but she couldn't deny herself a few toys every once in a while. She had the connections to get them, so what was there to lose?

From the nearby kitchen window, she could tell the day was nearly over. Michael, Aron, and Benedict were probably still up on the mountain, enjoying a much better view than she had.

She found bliss at the bottom of a bag of Doritos as night came, lying back on the worn couch watching a cheesy SyFy Channel movie about some giant mechanical spiders terrorizing women in bikinis. She never once considered her position unflattering. She was who she was, with the looks of a retired model and the personality and interests of a twelve-year-old. And she knew it, too, and was proud of it.

Continuing to indulge herself, she didn't bother jumping to her purse when she heard the low humming of her phone vibrating inside. She let it go; her phone was only set to vibrate for unknown callers, and she wasn't willing to put herself through any more nonsense. Since early that summer, she had been plagued with crank call after crank call, deep and sometimes electronic voices rattling off numbers in what sounded like Spanish. Not wanting to subject herself to any more pointless calls, she elected to let the caller leave a voicemail.

Soon after the ringing stopped, a second call came through, then a third as her patience wore thin. The constant repetition wasn't typical of the crank calls. Growing annoyed, Andrea retrieved her purse from the Predator's raised hand and looked at the missed calls.

All of them had come from a Colorado area code, but none she recognized. The only number she had on her phone from Colorado was Benedict, and since his ringtone —Shia LaBeouf screaming, *"JUST DO IT!"*—wasn't playing, she reluctantly answered the fourth call.

"Yes?" she asked, before a heavy, unfamiliar voice smothered hers.

"Benedict is dying. He is at Desert Regional Medical Center. Others are on the move. Hurry."

With a click, the line went dead.

26

"WHAT THE HELL WAS THAT?" DAVID ROARED AS HE THREW HIS HELMET TO THE GROUND.

After forcing their way out of the station, the brothers had stolen mountain bikes from the ranger cabin and rushed down the mountain, keeping to whatever clearings and paths they could. They still had a long way to go, but they found an isolated ravine two thirds of the way down, and chose to rest there until night fell.

They misled bystanders by first heading up the mountain trail, making it look like they would be hiding out deep in the forest. But after they were well out of sight, they changed course and headed down the mountain. It didn't look like a search was on yet, but they had no doubt their time was limited.

The rescue services at the fallen tram car had been on the scene within minutes. When the first helicopter landed, they knew any hope of securing Benedict was lost. An army of police cars and trucks soon followed, and David knew they had no option but to hide. They could cross the barren desert at night without as much risk.

The brothers had watched carefully from a distance, seeing the rescue team load four gurneys onto the chopper before flying off towards town at record speed. If everyone had died, there wouldn't have been as much of a rush to get back to town, so at least one of the tram car's occupants had survived. There was still hope, but David wasn't taking the loss well. He had bottled all his anger until he and Evans were miles away from the crash site and search area. Now, with no one in earshot, he'd let loose.

"I was trying to stop the tram from going any further," Evans began, "but—"

"Well, that worked out *real* well, didn't it?" David shouted, making no effort to keep his voice down.

"No, it didn't. It could have if you'd done what I told you!"

"What's that supposed to mean?"

"I was waiting for you to show up," Evans replied. "You knew I had a bad hand. The only reason I could shoot that guard was because I was right behind him!"

David growled. "So you ruined our last chance because you didn't want to aim with your left hand?"

"We were both shooting at the damned thing, how do I know it wasn't your bullet that—?"

Evans never got the chance to finish.

David swung and landed a solid punch to his brother's unprotected jaw, sending him flailing to the ground as a distorted swear left his lips. David was furious, not far from foaming at the mouth himself as he watched Evans fall, knowing he was probably right.

While his memory of the moment had been faint, he distinctly remembered aiming too high, far above the intended target of the control box. He wasn't thinking. In the moment, his panic had taken over and won.

"I know it didn't work. You don't have to remind me." Now, David made a conscious effort to keep his voice down.

Evans briefly tried to sit up before succumbing to a coughing fit. Covering his mouth with his left hand, the wet coughs came and went, leaving a bloody smear on Evans's palm. He froze in disbelief, staring up at his brother.

They hadn't gone out of their way to hurt each other since they were kids, and now neither of them was sure what to make of it.

But as he stared down at his brother, David knew. He might have brought the coughing fit on, but his strike was nowhere near enough to cause bleeding.

Evans's internal injuries were catching up with him.

They were being pushed to their breaking point. At every turn, their plans had fallen apart, and it was only be a matter of time before the wrong people caught up with them. How were they supposed to react? The longer they fought in their father's crusade, the more separated David became from his sense of rationality. His military training was slipping through his fingers, taking reason with it.

David extended a hand to his brother and helped him

to his feet, their eyes locked the whole way up. They both knew that they couldn't keep fighting each other or arguing over what went wrong. They needed to focus and move on.

But what was there left to do? Just head into the hospital, guns blazing? It would be suicide to attempt anything so straightforward again.

Not to mention impractical if Benedict was already dead.

27

ANDREA BURST INTO THE EMERGENCY ROOM, SEARCHING FRANTICALLY FOR SOMEONE TO HELP HER.

She hurried to the front desk, where she was greeted by a preoccupied nurse who didn't want anything to do with her. However, Andrea's worst fear was confirmed when the nurse told her that Aron and Michael were upstairs in intensive care, although she didn't know where Benedict was being held. That was all the information Andrea could get before the nurse placed a band on her wrist and sent her on her way, giving rough directions to their rooms.

Andrea crammed herself into an already packed elevator and made the ascent to Michael and Aron's floor. Making a mad dash out as the doors opened, she went to Michael's room first, since it was the closest. But the glass door was locked, and at least five nurses were gathered around his bedside. What few glimpses she got of him were not good: His face was cut up and bruised, he looked heavily drugged, and he didn't look comfortable at all.

Andrea caught a nurse going into the room, but she said she could only give information to Michael's family before closing the door in Andrea's face. She wanted to stay by him, to see if he was going to be all right or if she was about to watch him...

No, she couldn't think like that.

She forced herself to move on. She found Aron's room a few doors down with only one nurse tending to him. He was awake, but he didn't seem much better off than Michael. A thick stripe of blood soaked through the bandages wrapped around his left arm. He was also drugged, but he appeared to be more aware of his surroundings than Michael was.

When Aron looked over and saw her, his eyes widened.

"Benedict..." Aron slurred. "301... they're taking him."

Before the nurse could ask who she was, and before Aron could say any more, Andrea looked down the hall to see a gurney being wheeled away by two men dressed in black military garb. She raced toward them, ready to fight if these were the terrorists that Michael feared had survived the helicopter crash.

She spun one around, only to find that he obviously wasn't one of the steroid-filled jocks. Instead, he was a trim and somewhat handsome man who looked to be of Filipino descent. He looked shocked to see her, but the one who actually vocalized a reaction was Benedict, who lay on the gurney below, blood streaming from an unbandaged cut on his forehead.

"It's... okay. Taking... *Vulture*... back to..." he slurred, before trailing off. Andrea removed her grasp on the man who still looked shocked at her sudden appearance.

"You don't need to worry," the man said. "We're with DenCom. We were called to take Benedict to a secure facility for recovery."

"You're the 'others' that I was called about?" she asked.

The man looked perplexed, then gave a small laugh. "I guess Nelson's calling everyone. But that's right. I'm Dodgson, and this is Ferris." Dodgson motioned to the bulky man on the other end of the gurney. "We're following a plan laid out by Benedict."

"But how did you—?"

"I'm sorry, but we don't have much time," Dodgson said. "We need to get him somewhere safe. Just know that he and your friends will be all right. They're all in bad shape, but they should come out of it soon." He signaled for Ferris to move the cart through the busy hallway. "Call the crew and tell them we'll be ready in five. This is going to be one hell of a takeoff."

Andrea lost the two men and Benedict in the sea of activity, leaving her with too many questions to process as hospital staff raced around her.

28

IT WAS LATE THAT NIGHT WHEN DAVID AND EVANS RETURNED TO THE MOTEL. They rode the bikes until they were a mile out of town, at which time they left them behind and walked the last mile. Avoiding the main road, they walked down back streets and neighborhoods until they reached the motel.

David headed straight for the reading chair, not bothering to check the room for any signs of intrusion, while Evans lumbered into the bathroom to wash his mouth out. Over the ride back, Evans had been forced to stop on three occasions to cough his lungs out, always ending the fit with a bloody splotch in his hand.

As the sun rose and engulfed the room in light, David couldn't help but sit back and take in the rare silence.

The dreadful, telling silence.

David hesitated, not wanting to face the truth. Finally, he looked over at Erickson's still form on the bed, his skin already growing dark and lifeless. A full minute passed as David stared at the corpse, the silence only broken by the splashes of water from the bathroom.

He knew he should be crying, but he couldn't bring himself to tears. In the open-mouthed face on the bed, David saw his beloved twin brother, who had been his biggest inspiration for as long as he could remember. Always the strongest and toughest of them, Erickson had been the born leader that David had admired since childhood. They had fought, but they had loved each other as brothers should; the beatings and bruises reminders that they wouldn't have been so harsh on one another if they didn't care. David could hear him in the distance: A young boy laughing, sitting atop a dingy old playground in rural Ohio, proclaiming himself king of the world.

David heard Evans walk back into the room, but he didn't bother acknowledging him. He only stared at the body on the bed, uttering the only confirmation Evans needed.

"At least you're with Mom, now."

Suddenly, David raised his hand and brought it down on the wooden armrest with brute strength that would have made an older Erickson proud. The armrest snapped like a twig, breaking at both bases, dangling from the side of the chair by several frail tendons of wood.

David didn't notice the damage he'd done, but he did notice something foreign, something he hadn't felt in months:

Pain.

He grimly realized that it had been a week since their last NS injection.

"Get the syringes," David ordered.

Evans wandered over to their bag and retrieved a small, black plastic box, his eyes never leaving Erickson as he did so.

David flipped open the box and stared down at the three needles inside. The dosage they took before they left had been intended to cover the whole operation, but they'd brought an extra week's worth, just in case.

In an act that had become routine, David popped the cap off the syringe and headed for the mirror near the television. Once he had a clear shot, he sank the needle into the carotid artery, slowly pushing the clear liquid into his bloodstream. Evans grabbed his own syringe and headed for the bathroom, no doubt to do the same.

Once the clear liquid was gone, David carefully removed the syringe, reached for the tissue box, and used a tissue to apply pressure, stopping what little bleeding there may have been. Setting the syringe on the TV stand for later disposal, away from the prying eyes of motel staff, David returned to the partially destroyed chair.

Two attacks had failed to capture Benedict. Now, they were a man down—a brother down—and he knew Evans would probably be next if they didn't get help soon.

Their father had the technology back home to make them both well. He could bring in doctors who could help. But here, their support was almost nonexistent. The delivery they had received was the most their available backers would give; any more would risk revealing them. Unless they could get home or their father could pay someone off to help, the brothers were out of options.

David wondered if things would have turned out differently if they hadn't joined the military. Maybe then, their father wouldn't have expected so much from them. If David had held firm against his brothers' plans, maybe he would be in front of a desk right now, utilizing the coding skill he'd inherited from their father. It would have been a much quieter life, but it would have been his.

This thing he called life now, though, was far from his own.

But it was all he had. Choices had been made: Family over future, over happiness.

It was Evans's turn to keep watch, but David refused to let him. Evans needed rest; it was clear his deteriorating body was being pushed to its limits. He asked David if they should take care of Erickson now, but David couldn't think of what to do with him yet, especially in broad daylight. For the moment, all they could do was cover their deceased brother with a few blankets and unplug the medical equipment that couldn't help him anymore.

David thought that Erickson looked strangely at peace, like a sudden move could wake him up. Of course, if they did wake him up, they'd probably both get a punch in the gut.

Just the way it should have been. A small, sad laugh escaped David's lips.

After convincing Evans to take the second bed, David lay back in the reading chair and turned on the local news, careful to keep the volume low.

The bulky, finicky motel TV was at least twenty years old, but David could still make out an aerial view of the crash site, however garnished with static. Below, the tram car was brightly illuminated by ground lights. Fire trucks and police cars swarmed the wreck like flies on roadkill, looking for evidence of what had happened. They had flipped the car over to inspect it, but David knew they were looking in the wrong place. The metal support, still buried in the rubble of the station with the second car, was where they would have any chance finding anything traceable.

From there, the story shifted its focus to the families still stuck at the top of the mountain. The only way down was via helicopter, and that was going slowly, at best. There were approximately three hundred people, perhaps more, stuck up there, and with the helicopters only able to take five or so people at a time, the vast majority would be up there a while. At best, everyone would be down in a day or two, so the news had something to occupy people's time while they were waiting for security camera footage.

It was unavoidable that they had been captured on film, by security cameras or otherwise. Normally, the news networks would have had something by now, but they didn't, and it was clear to David why:

The President was facing a credibility nightmare.

The government had blatantly lied about the brothers' escape, telling people that the crash and resulting fire were merely due to a downed personal aircraft. They had provided the media with a fabricated story, insisting that the terrorists were still in custody, in the hopes of buying time to recapture them before people went into a panic.

But now it would be obvious, even on the low-quality security cameras, that the attackers at the Spectrum had, in fact, resurfaced at the Skyway Tram, albeit short one member. It would be nearly impossible to admit to the public with a straight face that the government had knowingly lied about terrorist activities within the country.

As the news anchor went on about the crash, she was suddenly handed a new update. She announced that, thankfully, everyone in the car had survived the crash, but they were all in critical condition. Their names had yet to be released, but David had heard enough.

They had made it out. There was still a chance to get Benedict. For one moment of bliss, David left his anger behind.

But the trance was quickly broken as his cell phone rang. He looked down at the caller ID with disgust but wasted no time picking it up.

"Father?"

"What happened?"

David recounted the story and confirmed that Benedict was still alive before his father cut him off.

"I know. I have the feed." He sighed. "I thought this would be a simple enough task for you three."

David felt his fist involuntarily clench around the

phone, nearly snapping the plastic device in two. "With all due respect, Father, there are only two of us now. Erickson's *dead*! Do you hear me? Do you understand what I'm saying?" His voice was nearing a roar. "He was dead when we got back. He's gone! Your son is *dead* because of *your* vendetta, and we didn't do anything useful to help him!"

"You mean *I* didn't do anything useful, right?" he growled.

"Yes, Father, that is *exactly* what I'm saying," David replied bitterly. He was taking his frustration out on the one man who deserved it above all others. He wanted to make it clear that he was not right for this job, that he was no more a soldier than Erickson had been a saint. David wanted to tell his father that if he wanted to hit DenCom so badly, he should get off his wheelchaired ass and catch Benedict himself, instead of spending all his time staring at monitors, hoping to make sense out of the static. He wanted to tell the beaten, bitter old man to go straight to Hell.

David looked over to see Evans awake and signaling for him to stop protesting. The consequences would be too great to risk.

But to their surprise, their father agreed. "I suppose I didn't, but you two are the only ones who can change that now."

"All right, but what *can* we do?" David asked, only growing more irritated.

"Why don't you just ask *Benedict* for some help?"

29

Saturday, July 27th
Desert Regional Medical Center
Palm Springs, California
11:07 AM

A FAMILIAR WHITE LIGHT SMOTHERED MICHAEL AS HE SLOWLY WOKE UP. As it faded, he could make out an IV drip above his head and several monitors on either side of him. It was a sight he had unwillingly become used to; this was his second hospital room in two days.

Or had it been longer?

It felt longer.

He couldn't figure out why, but his body felt strangely rested. At least, until he moved. He groaned as he rolled over, but before he could do much, the blurry form of Andrea appeared above him, and he settled back down onto the bed.

"Morning, Sunshine," she said, sounding miles away.

Michael instinctively reached to adjust his hearing aid but felt nothing. Andrea held up a finger as she picked up the small device from the table on Michael's left and placed it snugly in his left ear before he could find the strength to move.

"Sorry," she said, pulling her hand away. "They had to

take it out when you came in. How're you feeling?"

The words came out slowly, groggily. "You ever... you ever see a hamster in a wheel lose control and get flung out? I kinda feel like that."

Andrea let out a small laugh. "You sound like Benedict. But you're not that far off. How much do you remember?"

Michael closed his eyes, thinking back to the most recent attack on his life. "I remember getting in the car and when it started to lose control. After it hit the last tower, my memory's fuzzy."

Andrea nodded. "Emergency services found the car just outside the parking area off the road. No one was thrown out, but none of you were in great shape."

Michael tried to sit up straight but found that his body wouldn't allow for much more than tilting his head.

"I wouldn't try much right now," Andrea said. "You're pretty drugged."

Michael reluctantly obliged. "How are the others?"

"Aron and the tram driver are awake. Both have a lot of cuts, but Aron has a cracked rib and a large gash on his arm. The doctors may release him today, but his arm will be in a sling for a while. And Benedict... Well, from what I understand, he was taken to a secure DenCom location. We don't know where he is, but he wasn't looking good. People from DenCom showed up right after the crash and took him away, saying they were following a plan that Benedict had put in place."

"You sure it was DenCom?" Michael asked.

"I hope so. Benedict was awake enough to say it was okay, but he didn't say much else."

Michael wasn't sure what to think of this new development. He knew that Benedict had precautions in place, such as the secure hospital in Irvine, for if he was severely injured and away from home. Whether or not that was where he'd been taken was anyone's guess.

"All right, how are things looking for me?" Michael asked.

"Two cracked ribs, and some other internal problems I don't know the specifics on. They say none of it needs surgery, but there's no doubt it's going to hurt like hell. I know they want you to stay in bed, but whether here or at home, I don't know," she said.

"You really think they'll let me go?" he asked.

"Well, Aron is probably checking out today, and the tram driver's already gone, so maybe. By the way, she said to thank you for the advice. It saved your lives, but she doesn't want anything more to do with us."

"Don't blame her," Michael said.

"Me neither, but anyway, as far as you go, I can't say for sure. Honestly, I had to verbally beat them for information since I'm not family."

Michael's heart skipped a beat. He hadn't even thought about it. "Does my family know what happened?"

"I... I don't know. If they do, I didn't tell them."

They both knew Michael wasn't on good terms with most of his family. If any of them would have shown up, it would have been Mark, and he would no doubt tell their parents, who would freak out and fly in. It would end up being a huge waste of money that would do little to ease the tension. Michael sighed; he knew it wasn't right to keep them out of the loop, but it was best for everyone involved.

"It's all right," Michael said. "I can deal with it if it comes."

"Okay, you want me to get the doctor?" she asked.

He said he did, and Andrea left the room.

Once she was out of sight, Michael tried to move his hands and found they were numb but still responsive. He reached for the television remote and flipped on the news.

An anchorwoman wearing too much makeup was recounting the story of the tram crash and referring to it as a terrorist attack. She said it was unknown if this attack was related the one in Irvine but mentioned that police were looking into it. She then switched over to a recount of a local UFO sighting a few nights ago.

The tram coverage depressed him to no end, so he flipped on his favorite time-wasting station, the Weather Channel. It was a tradition for him to let it play in the background when he traveled or was stuck in a hotel, although it always made him depressed that he hadn't minored in meteorology back in college.

Before the familiar self-loathing could go any farther, Andrea brought the doctor in. He was a generic, Mr. Fantastic-type Touch of Gray spokesman with a trim, thin face. Michael muted the TV as the doctor sat in a chair next to his bed.

They exchanged the general questions on how Michael was feeling and exactly what had happened to him. The doctor explained that the damage was no longer life-threatening, but it easily could have been. He treated his survival, as well as that of the other occupants, as a miracle.

To keep the pain down, the doctor planned to prescribe pills that would keep the pain at bay, for the most part. He was also the first to tell Michael that he had been asleep for three days, kept under for his own safety while his body naturally recovered. The only question Michael had left was if Granger was okay.

"I've been staying at your place for the last few days," Andrea assured him. "Granger and the fish are all doing fine. Aron let me borrow his room, since I felt bad leaving Granger there all by herself."

"Thanks, but would you mind staying another day, since I'm apparently going to be stuck here? I'm guessing Aron can't do much."

"Are you kidding? Of course, I don't mind. Granger's been great. Not to mention it'll give us an excuse to catch up on our shows," Andrea replied, and Michael felt a weight he didn't even know was there lift off his shoulders.

"Thanks, and take my bed, so you don't have to sleep on the couch when Aron gets back."

"Only if Granger can join me."

Michael couldn't help but smile at her enthusiasm. He was glad someone else cared about Granger as much as he and Aron did. "All right, but don't give her any ideas. When I'm home, she's back in the living room."

"Can do. It'll be our little secret."

The doctor then rehashed the same information that Andrea had given him about the others but included one new development.

"We've been in contact with DenCom Medical, the facility where your friend Benedict was taken. He's doing well, but he's hoping to hear from you. He's on the phone with Aron now. When they're done, do you want me to see if we can have the call transferred here?"

"Sounds fine to me," Michael replied.

As the doctor started to leave with Andrea, he mentioned that the call would be put through momentarily.

Michael held the silent phone to his ear, waiting for the elevator music to end and for Benedict to come on the line. But what was going to come of it? After the terrorists' second attack—the attack that Michael had predicted and taken the time to warn Benedict about—would Benedict own up to his lack of foresight? Or would he claim that he had been right all along and that they needed to "relax" again?

Even before Benedict answered, Michael knew what he was going to say, and this time, he was prepared.

"Michael?"

"Yeah, I'm here. Just woke up."

"Oh, thank God. Listen, I'm sorry if I freaked you guys out by leaving, but I feel terrible that I couldn't take you with me. Protocol hadn't accounted for more than one person, and I was too out of it to—"

Michael cut off the painful excuse. "You don't have to explain. I'm glad I'm still close to home."

"Good to hear. So, how are you?"

Michael gave him the general rundown.

"Yeah, you sound better than they thought you would be. They were talking surgery when you first came in, from what I heard," Benedict said.

"Maybe I did have surgery."

"You don't know?"

"There's a lot I don't know, Benedict."

Silence.

"Well, what do you know?"

"First of all, I know I told you we weren't safe," Michael snapped. "I know I told you that they were probably coming for us, and that we needed to do something about it. And I know that it did not cross your mind, not even for one second, that there was even a minute possibility of me being right until it was too late."

Shuffling filled the other end of the line. Benedict was probably sitting up in his own hospital bed, an assumption that was confirmed as Michael heard Benedict's muffled voice advise a nurse not to stop him.

"You really expected me to believe they survived?" Benedict retorted after some more shuffling from the other end.

"No, I thought you would believe me when I said I was almost *murdered* at the Spectrum! So, you were wrong twice over."

"Was I supposed to just assume they survived the helicopter crash?"

"No, you were supposed to assume we were in danger because of our connection to DenCom, based on the fact that—again—I was almost murdered! And, quite frankly, I'd like to hear you explain *that* side of it. Why are we targets?"

"You mean why *were* you targets."

Michael's jaw dropped. He couldn't believe it. Once again, Benedict was trying to brush off future risks of attack, even though this time, they knew for *certain* that the terrorists were still out there.

"But these guys—"

"—aren't going to do anything until things cool off," Benedict calmly finished. "The tram station provided better visuals of the attackers that were impossible to cover up, and witnesses of the Spectrum attack are saying that those were the same guys. On top of that, the media's also going after the President, who approved the government's obvious cover-up to prevent a panic.

"But now, it *is* a panic, one that *you're* perpetuating. I keep reading about lookalike arrests and how people are worried that another attack could happen at any time. But here's the reality: The President and I think the worst of the danger has passed. It's been three days since the terrorists fled the scene. There's an ongoing search to find them, but nothing's come up. They know they've screwed up, so they've gone into hiding, and sooner or later, we'll find them, and this can finally be over."

"And I'm guessing the President also told you that there was no possibility of a second attack."

Benedict was silent.

"Listen," Michael continued, "there is no way I'm going to trust your judgment right now. We know they're still out there, still waiting for one of us to screw up, and don't waste your breath telling me otherwise. If this is because of the work Aron and I have done for DenCom, then we need DenCom's protection."

"Meaning?"

"I want to be taken to a safe house, Aron too if he'll go along with it. I want twenty-four-seven, high-priority protection until someone competent puts a bullet through these terrorists' heads. I don't care how long it takes or how much money it costs you, I want the protection DenCom has denied us thus far."

The line grew quiet. There was more shuffling, as if Benedict had his hand over the receiver. Michael tapped his numb fingers on the bed, waiting a full minute before Benedict came on the line again.

"I can have your house put under surveillance by local police, possibly the FBI if they have anyone to spare. As far as the hospital goes, they have their own security to guard you."

"They any better than the ones at that Irvine hospital?"

"Let's hope so."

"And no safe house?"

"None you'd appreciate."

Michael processed the insult, if that's what it truly was. "A few beat cops are supposed to make me feel safe?"

The caustic remark seemed to go over Benedict's head. "They can be there tonight, so I'm told. I can also have them search the condo, just in case our friends have been by. If you think Granger would tolerate it, that is."

"She'll have to."

"So, that'll work for you?"

"It'll have to, since that's all you're offering."

"It's all I'm allowed, at the moment."

"What do you mean?"

More shuffling. This time, only half a minute passed before Benedict returned to the line.

"They'll be there tonight to watch over Aron, and I'll see if I can't get someone over at Andrea's. When're you checking out?"

"Tomorrow morning, so I'm told."

"All right, I'll fly in sometime in the afternoon to see you."

"You sure that's wise?" Michael asked sardonically.

"If it helps you, I don't care. I'll come by, and we can talk over any further involvement you wish to have with DenCom."

"If *any.*"

Benedict sighed. "We'll see."

The line clicked off, and Michael took in a deep, much needed breath before setting the phone back on the table.

30

Sunday, July 28th
Desert Regional Medical Center
Palm Springs, California
12:22 AM

MICHAEL BRIEFLY MET WITH ARON BEFORE ANDREA DROVE HIM HOME. Aron planned on retreating to his room when they got home, giving Andrea and Granger free roam of the house, which Michael supported.

Aron left the hospital in a wheelchair—more for insurance reasons than anything else, since he could walk just fine—with his left arm in a sling. He wouldn't be able to grasp anything or do much with the arm for a while, but if Michael knew Aron as well as he thought he did, he suspected he would never see the sling again once his friend was out of the doctor's sight.

Otherwise, Aron looked fine, aside from several cuts and bruises on his face and lower neck. And, of course, the inevitable scar that would form on his arm, which didn't seem to bother him. As he left with Andrea, he joked that maybe the cuts and bruises would make him a chick magnet, at which Andrea rolled her eyes.

The subject of DenCom had been actively—and intentionally—ignored.

That night, the doctor offered to put Michael under for observation reasons, but he declined in favor of late night television and his thoughts. Hours passed as he flipped between the Weather Channel and a marathon of *The Golden Girls.*

Over the course of the night, Michael couldn't stop thinking about the accident, which made him tempted to call the doctor back in and say he had changed his mind about staying up. At the moment, he wasn't mentally or physically capable of handling the problem, but the questions kept sneaking into his head: Who were they? What did they want from him? What would be their next move?

Michael got his answer when his bedside phone rang.

"Mr. Ridding, you have a guest here to see you," the receptionist on the other end said.

Michael groaned. "This late? Who is it?"

"He says he's your brother, Mark."

Damn it. The battle for his privacy was lost before it had even started. Now that Mark was in the picture, his parents wouldn't be far behind. But he didn't have the heart to turn his brother away, despite the inevitable train wreck that would follow.

Swallowing his pride, he told the receptionist that it was fine to let Mark up. In those grueling few minutes he waited, Michael tried to make himself look presentable, or at least as presentable as the various sensors and needles in his arms allowed. Soon, he heard elevator doors open nearby, followed by the echo of heavy bootsteps in the deserted hallway. He muted the TV, never expecting one of the terrorists to be standing in the doorway when he looked back.

The killer had grown a good stubble of beard—not surprising, given that Michael had been asleep for three days. He had slicked back his now jet-black hair, and his outfit was far more casual: A Slayer t-shirt and blue denim pants.

"Hello, Mr. Ridding," the man said with just a hint of an accent Michael couldn't place. "Don't bother getting up."

He took a seat where the doctor had been only a few hours ago and studied his prey's beaten body.

Michael tensed. Why was this man here? Was he about to finish what he had started?

"Impressive," the man said. "I thought you would've died in that crash, but you're all tougher than we thought. But that doesn't matter right now. What matters is that until we can get our hands on Benedict, you'll have to do."

Michael lunged toward the assistance button with what strength and speed he had, but before he could press it, the man caught his wrist with a strong, firm grip, trapping it only inches away from its goal. They both knew he was only using minimal strength to hold Michael back, but that didn't deter him.

"You don't want to do that," the man snarled. "If you do, I guarantee you'll be dead before anyone shows up. Which would be tragic since, as it happens, you may be of some use to us."

Against his better judgment, Michael stopped fighting, and the man let Michael's hand fall back to his side. It was clear that the man wasn't messing around—hadn't been from the start—but Michael could sense that both parties wished to avoid violence during this meeting.

"Listen, I don't know you, but—"

"David. You can call me David."

"All right, David," Michael said. "I guess I should start by saying that you have a lot of explaining to do."

"I'm sure we all do, including your little group of truth-seekers," David replied. "I'm here to propose a cease-fire of sorts. I believe I have information that will convince you to sympathize with us and, hopefully, help bring this violence to an end."

"All right," Michael said, masking his fear with skepticism. "But why come to me with this? Why now, after so many people died? I have no authority; I can't get the government to stop hunting you. Shouldn't you go to them with your compromise?"

David wasted no time answering. "The government would never go along with what we're proposing, since they already have enough cover-ups on their plate. Besides, you're in the best position to get us what we're looking for."

"Which is?"

"Benedict," David growled. "We need your cooperation to capture him and take him to our father. There, he'll be punished for his sins against humanity."

Michael was floored. He knew Benedict had to have

done *something* bad to draw the terrorists' attention, but sins against humanity? That was pushing it.

He wanted to say no, to just end the conversation there and move on. But Michael had a feeling that if he did, he wouldn't live to see the man leave.

"Why should I help you do anything to my employer, not to mention my friend?"

David laughed, seeing right through Michael's pitiful attempt at bravery. Then, as if possessed, he got down to business.

"Because none of you know who he truly is and what he's capable of. He is, in a sense, one of the most powerful men on Earth, and you all seem to be completely ignorant of that. You, your President, and in turn, the rest of the world are his puppets. You've ignored the atrocities that Benedict has been a party to, or even facilitated. Instead, you choose to take him as some sort of clown, some sort of harmless nutjob. And that's why I'm here now, to tell you what Benedict doesn't want you to know about him. All the secrets he's kept from you and from the public— everything you should've already been told."

Michael was unconvinced. He didn't want to listen, but knew the alternative was far more unsavory. For now, he was a captive audience. There was no point in fighting it.

"All right, let's hear it," Michael said. "What exactly has Benedict done that you think is worth all this?"

David smiled, then recited his piece.

31

"AS IS KNOWN THROUGHOUT CONSPIRACY GROUPS, BENEDICT IS IN A CONSTANT SEARCH FOR THE WORLD'S TRUTHS. Using DenCom's resources, as well as the occasional favor from the government, he facilitates ongoing investigations regarding a multitude of unknown topics. It's widely believed he's searched for Sasquatch, aliens, religious relics, and God only knows what else. But we have reason to believe that Benedict knows more through his research, private investigators, and government connections than any of you know.

"I can tell you that my father, the man who sent us on this mission, once worked for DenCom as a network administrator, a much lower-tier position than you're in. He approached Benedict about a case, and Benedict nearly killed him for it. My father was not forceful or aggressive; he simply wished to know the truth about something that had been plaguing his dreams for years. But Benedict told him that that was beyond him, that what he wanted to know was the same thing that had driven himself to near insanity. Their confrontation ended with Benedict *torturing* my father for information, since there was one thing he had that Benedict never did: The visions.

"My father claimed to have visions of a battle from the distant past, a battle where two of God's angels fought in a valley of golden fire. He said the images were terrifying, yet strangely inspiring. The kind of thing that, to quote him, was 'so awesome in magnitude and so terrible in scope that it could only be the work of God'. He was plagued by this vision, as well as visits from one apparition in particular: A demonic form, a being he described as a decrepit skeleton cowboy who stood over his bed. He would wake to find it screaming at him, its hollow eyes staring into the rawest part of his soul.

"After years of suffering, my father went to Benedict for answers, but he kept refusing to take his calls. Then, after a particularly intense encounter, my father snapped. He thought that Benedict was deliberately avoiding him, thinking he was just some nutjob, some pest who would eventually get bored and stop harassing him. After all, at DenCom, he was just another faceless IT guy—what did he know about the paranormal? But my father was determined to get his answers, since he had a feeling Benedict knew more than he was letting on. And maybe my father was a nutjob after all, or even still is. But at this point, I don't think I care anymore. I just care about what happened next.

"When my father burst into Benedict's office and tried to explain what happened, Benedict had security knock him out and take him away. He later woke in a dark room, where Benedict and another man nearly killed him for asking too much. *He* gave every order, every approval to rip skin from flesh, stab him, inject him, and eventually burn most of his skin off with acid. But Benedict never got his hands dirty; the other man did most of the work. He only asked questions my father didn't know the answers to, and every time my father demanded the truth, he was punished for it.

"He never got his answers, but he did learn that Benedict knew enough to consider my father a threat. What Benedict said was burned into my father's memory, but he only shared it with me once. He said: 'You have seen the Valley, and I envy you. However, this is not something that needs to be made public. There is so much like this battle that the world should never know about. If it did, our churches would be filled with lies, the people constantly in question of their own morality. It is imperative to keep the insanity and lost feelings alive in our society, and you are a threat to the chaos. As such, you're going to disappear *very* soon, and if I were you, I would never mention the Valley to anyone else for as long as you live. Your worthless life depends on it.'

"Soon after, while my father was still in recovery, he was exiled to our grandfather's old hunting cabin in Greenland. It was remote, abandoned, and falling apart—the perfect place to hide him so Benedict could cover his own ass. They gave him enough drugs and food for a month, but after that, any help from DenCom was gone. Benedict just left him there to die.

"My father had no way to communicate with the outside world. We were in Iraq doing a tour when we got word that our father hadn't been heard from in months. DenCom wouldn't comment, his apartment looked untouched... for all intents and purposes, he'd vanished into thin air. We thought he'd died, and it was widely assumed that our sister's disappearance had finally gotten to him. Then, we received a letter from a private organization based in Russia. They claimed to have helped my father after finding him in Greenland, and after tracking us down, they wanted our help, too.

"With help from our new supporters, we worked out a staged bombing to fake our deaths. From there, we were flown to Greenland to see our father for the first time in years. He explained what happened to him, and that these people also had a vendetta against DenCom and Benedict. That was where their common views ended, though, but it was still enough to convince him to work with them. Even if they turned out to be as seedy as DenCom, they were still a blessing to us, and we wanted to uphold our end of the bargain. So, over the years, they built us back up to where we were and made us who we are today. They gave us everything we needed to become efficient soldiers, from further training to steroids and nerve suppressors. And together, we formulated a plan to capture Benedict.

"It took years to put in motion. Initially, they had hoped it would be a matter of hacking into DenCom's servers and stealing as much data as they could. My father used his extensive knowledge of the company's network infrastructure, as well as the resources given to him by the Russian organization, but he found nothing regarding his visions—or anything relating to DenCom's cryptic investigations, for that matter. Eventually, though, he tracked down an old e-mail from a jeweler in New York.

On the surface, it looked like nothing, but we believe it's the key.

"The e-mail detailed a special necklace that was crafted specifically for Benedict. Supposedly, there is a flash drive hidden inside that we are convinced contains a copy—possibly the *only* copy—of his investigation files. The world's secrets are *all* hidden on that flash drive, and Benedict wears it like a trophy.

"We know we've done awful things to get it, but I need to know, my brother gave his *life* to know, and my father *deserves* to know. And you and your loved ones should be equally curious, given what *he's* put you through. It doesn't matter if you see him as your friend— if, one day, you ever tried to get the truth from *him*, Benedict would dispose of you just as easily and casually as he disposed of my father.

"So I offer you a compromise that could end this fight forever. According to trusted sources, the *Bluestream* is heading to Palm Springs tomorrow. Benedict will almost certainly be on board, and it's my educated guess that he'll be coming to visit you. When he does, I need you to... *convince* him to fly you, as well as me and my brother, to our home in Greenland. There, we can recover, my father can confront Benedict, and our family can finally have some closure. Remember, bring Benedict *alone*, and tell no one else where we're going or what we're doing there.

"We will not be watching or listening in; getting past the guards you no doubt have waiting at your home wouldn't be worth the risk. Besides, I trust that you understand the consequences. You might be out of reach, but it'll be a piece of cake to find out more about your family than just your brother's name. If you disobey us—if you *fail*—we might just have to pay them a visit."

David pulled out a small, folded piece of paper and handed it to Michael, who limply took it.

"I'll be waiting for your call. Once you've secured Benedict, have him ready the *Bluestream* for takeoff. My brother and I will meet you at the hangar. Once we have him and the pendant, you'll come with us to Greenland, where you'll be among the first to see what Benedict has hidden from us all. Once he's out of the way, our benefactors can move in and do as they please. My father's revenge will be complete, and you, as well as your friends and family, will be pardoned for DenCom's crimes. But of course," David added, "it's your choice if you want to side with a madman."

He stood up and headed for the door.

"If I don't hear from you within two days, we'll assume you've sided with him. In that case, you'll also find out what it's like to lose a brother. Do I make myself clear?"

Michael weakly nodded.

"Have a nice night."

David rounded the corner into the hall and out of sight, the fading bootsteps echoing until the elevator doors opened and closed.

Michael couldn't bring himself to look at the card dangling between his fingers. All he could do was stare sightlessly at the TV above him as the weather forecast silently crawled across the bottom of the screen.

More storms were rolling in from across the Pacific.

32

THE DOCTOR WOKE MICHAEL THE FOLLOWING MORNING AND TOLD HIM HE COULD GO HOME, BUT NOT WITHOUT REMINDING HIM TO STAY IN BED AND TAKE IT EASY. If he was feeling better within the week, he could then resume his day-to-day activities. If not, they could look into other options.

Aron picked Michael up as soon as he had gotten the call. The Pantera pulled up, freshly cleaned and waxed, as Michael lifted himself out of the wheelchair and onto his limp legs. Aron—his arm no longer in the sling, just as Michael had predicted—and a nurse helped him into the passenger's seat, although Aron was obviously struggling. After taking the driver's seat, Aron wasted no time getting them out of there.

"How's the arm?" Michael asked, noticing it lay limply at Aron's side while he drove with his right hand.

"Useless," he replied. "For now, at least."

Michael was tempted to ask Aron if he was sure he could drive, but he didn't want to risk offending his friend, since neither of them liked being physically held back. He chose to trust Aron's judgment, instead, even after several close calls on the short drive home.

Michael hadn't fallen asleep until four AM, and it showed: The beginnings of a beard were forming on his face, and darkness ringed his already tired-looking eyes. He needed time to recover.

More time than David had given.

He only had forty-eight hours to secure Benedict. He wanted to call David back and demand more time to think it over. He wanted to be in a better state of mind before confronting Benedict, but he knew David wouldn't budge. He'd get hostile at the fact that Michael was even asking.

He was a slave to David's will, and he didn't like it. But what if what David said was true, and DenCom and Benedict were actually in the wrong? He would be hard-pressed to believe that he was still one of the "good guys" if even half David's story proved to be true. Even after all David and his brothers had done, was it possible that the *terrorists* were the lesser of two evils?

The prospect alone made him feel sick.

Michael couldn't process the matter. These people had tried to kill him—twice. And both times, in their failure, they had taken innocent lives.

He wasn't so innocent. Given that David's story was true, at best, Michael was guilty by association; at worst, he was Benedict's oblivious puppet. He almost *wanted* to be punished if it turned out that their work had created monsters like David and his father.

If it was true, he was done living a lie. He didn't care how much money he made. If his work contributed to the death and pain that Benedict supposedly brought about...

Michael was done.

He couldn't take it anymore.

If Benedict visited tonight, he didn't know what he would do.

But he would have to do something.

He was tired. Tired of Benedict's secrecy, tired of living DenCom's lie, and tired of looking over his shoulder.

And he wanted Benedict to know that.

As the car turned into the gated parking lot, Michael didn't fail to notice the police car parked several spaces away, not far from their home with a decent view of the walkway.

At least Benedict had kept one of his promises.

Aron walked with Michael through the garden, then called Andrea to help them up the stairs. After a few minutes, she rushed down, but not before forcing a curious Granger away from the open door as she headed outside.

They stayed close as Michael ascended the stairs. Each step, even with Aron and Andrea's gentle assistance, brought with it the feeling that his ribs were digging into his side and repeatedly piercing his vital organs. The doctor had said that no permanent damage had occurred, but every step brought him closer and closer to doubting that.

Eventually, they made it to his room, where Michael asked to be left alone to rest for a while, promising to call if he needed anything. They obliged, but before they could shut the door, Granger squeezed between them and into the room, then gracefully laid parallel to the bed.

Aron and Andrea called and motioned for Granger to come back, but Michael waved them off and said it was all right for her to stay. They reluctantly left, but Granger never took her eyes off her master until he fell asleep.

33

LATER THAT NIGHT, MICHAEL WOKE FACE-DOWN IN BED, GRANGER STILL SOUND ASLEEP ON THE FLOOR RIGHT BESIDE HIM. He shifted, then reached for his cell phone. The first try, he flopped back onto the pillows, his arm falling limply over the side of the bed. Unsure if it was a result of the pain or his still fading sleep, he tried again to raise the still weak hand.

Granger ran to his aid, pressing her body against his arm. He wasn't sure if she was trying to push it back up or comfort him, but as feeling returned, he tried for the phone again. He was able to unlock it and look at the time: Just after seven-thirty. He'd slept nearly the whole day.

He lifted his legs over the side of the bed and was about to stand up when, to his shock, Granger whipped her head around and hissed at him.

He wasn't sure why the cat had suddenly gone cross until she started nudging his legs, pushing them back up toward the bed. He realized with some surprise that she didn't want him to get up. She knew he was hurt.

He sighed. This animal was too smart for him.

Groaning, he lifted his legs back onto the bed.

Before he could relax, though, he heard people in the other room, talking loudly and laughing.

Benedict's voice was among them.

Michael reached for the cell phone again, Granger watching to make sure he didn't try anything. He texted Aron that he was up and wanted to come out before replacing the phone on the dresser.

As Aron entered, Michael had just finished sliding his insurance into his back pocket and covering it with his shirt.

Andrea followed close behind, and under Granger's watchful eye, the two of them led Michael out of his room and down the short hallway.

Once in the living room, Michael saw Benedict sipping lemonade on the couch, his trench coat freshly pressed and his black, rectangular pendant glistening in the chandelier's light.

Through the slits in the blind-covered sliding doors, Michael could see the lights of the city. It was calm and clear outside, the perfect desert night for life as he knew it to end.

"Let me stand here."

Aron and Andrea looked at him, puzzled, but Michael shot them both a look that plunged the room into silence. Even Granger froze mid-stride on her way to the couch.

The two of them obeyed, releasing Michael. He placed one hand on the wall to steady himself and glared at

Benedict.

Everyone held their breath as Michael spoke, his words dripping with indignation.

"Last night," he started, "I had a visitor. He said his name was David, but he'd sneaked in claiming to be my brother. *He* is one of the men who are hunting us."

Everyone was petrified, exchanging uncomfortable glances as Michael gathered the strength to continue his story.

"He told me that he and his brothers were sent here to capture you, Benedict, so they could get your pendant —or, should I say, your flash drive."

Benedict's face went white as marble.

"He said you tortured his father before leaving him for dead in Greenland. He also said that what's stored on your 'pendant' could change the world as we know it."

"Do you... do you believe him?"

Michael hesitated. "I'm not sure, Benedict. But I believe that you've left us all in the dark, never adequately explaining what our work means. And you know, I never had a problem with it until now. Writing a paper here, collecting an artifact there, getting paid a million dollars a year to not ask questions. But that was *before* people were trying to *kill* us! Now, I'm done with the secrecy, I'm done with your tricks, I'm done with the missions, and I'm done with *you* until you give us answers! Tell us why our lives— and possibly our *family's* lives—are at stake, and why you've handled this threat so lightly from day one! If you so much as look at me wrong, or if I get the feeling you're not telling me everything, I won't hesitate to hand you over to David and his father."

The room fell silent, all eyes on Benedict.

"All right."

The Benedict that Michael met seven years ago—the crying, pathetic, spoiled child trying his best to suppress his true fear—was shining through again. Benedict shifted in the chair, visibly struggling to fight the child.

But Michael knew he would fail.

"I guess we'll be here a while."

34

MICHAEL SAT DOWN ON THE OPPOSITE END OF THE L-SHAPED COUCH. Aron and Andrea sat on the open end near the sliding glass doors, huddled together like a high school couple caught in the back seat of a car. Michael could tell they were frightened—they all were—but he couldn't worry about how they felt. It had to be done.

"Benedict, you've always been a good friend," Michael started, "but surely, you can agree that, over the past week, you've put all our lives at risk. I don't want to believe what I was told about you, but I'll do what I have to if they're right."

"You're armed, aren't you?" Benedict said with forced calmness.

Michael hadn't expected the question. "I might be."

"I see."

"Did you torture David's father?"

Benedict sighed. Michael scrutinized him as he spoke.

"His name is William von Gordon, but now he just goes by Von Gord," Benedict explained, looking to no one in particular as the words left him, smooth and nonchalant. "He was a network administrator at DenCom, a real scrawny, broad-rimmed glasses kind of guy who was trying to dig too deep into my personal investigations."

Michael glared at Benedict.

"Yes," he admitted after a long, tense moment. "I had him tortured. Burned the majority of his body off. I had it done by a former... associate who is no longer my concern."

No one moved. For the first time in their lengthy friendship, Benedict had managed to frighten everyone in the room, and he had done so like he'd just admitted he forgot to buy bread at the grocery store.

Aron and Andrea stared at him, wide-eyed and speechless.

"Why?" Michael asked.

He watched Benedict take a breath. He knew the man was about to deflect the question, but he let it come anyway.

"Michael, there are certain things that he wanted to know, things that, if they got out, would have an irreversible effect on our current understanding of religion. There would be reformation of faith all over the globe unlike anything we have ever seen, it would—"

"'Our churches would be filled with lies, the people constantly in question of their own morality,'" Michael finished. "Was that what you were going to say?"

Benedict had obviously not anticipated Michael knowing so much. Enough to accurately quote Von Gord's account, at least.

He hesitated. "Might've been."

"Then, spare us your notecards and just tell us the truth!"

"You know, I would just *love* to!" Benedict yelled,

turning to Michael. "I would *love* to give you guys all the answers you want, especially if it meant we could be friends again. But think about something for a second: If I had all the answers, would I need you to help me? No, I wouldn't."

Michael briefly considered this. On one hand, the rare grain of logic that the billionaire divulged was sound. However, Michael refused to believe that Benedict knew as little as he implied.

"That's bull, and we all know it! It's obvious you know more than we do. You just won't say anything."

"But you knew that going in, Michael. You *knew* I wouldn't always tell you if your investigations were successful."

"But seven *years*, Benedict. A million dollars a year for seven years for *possibly* failed investigations? You must be getting *something*."

"We're getting closer every day, but not close enough for me to feel confident giving you answers."

"Then you're saying you nearly killed a man because you didn't have those answers, and you thought *he* did?"

"That's not true!"

"Then tell me, what did he see? *What is the Valley*?"

Benedict froze.

Silence filled the room.

Then, in a blur, he began to throw a tantrum, locked in a mental battle for control. He drew himself into a rocking ball, hyperventilating, clutching at his hair as he rocked back and forth on the couch. Droplets of sweat rolled down his exposed neck. Michael could barely hear him muttering as he shook violently:

"I don't know, I-I *don't*. No. No. N-no, I don't know, d-d-*damn* you! I can't explain it, I can't c-c-c-*comprehend* it. I can't k-keep myself f-from..."

He threw his arms away from his face, nearly hitting Aron, revealing a twisted version of the man they'd all come to know. His face glowed red, and several tears streamed down his swollen cheeks. Then he roared:

"SHUT UP, *SHUT UP*! WHY C-CAN'T YOU JUST *SHUT THE HELL UP!*"

Benedict fell limp on the couch like he'd just had the wind knocked out of him, letting the cushions settle around his trembling body.

Andrea placed a hand over her mouth. Aron was the first and only one to approach him, placing a comforting hand on the man's shoulder.

Michael only stared, unsure of what to think anymore.

He'd just hit on something extremely personal, perhaps a mental trigger in the man's less-than-whole mind. They knew him as crazy, always trying to have fun whenever he could and being serious only when he needed to. But it was clear that he held back other tendencies, possible debilitating symptoms of a mental disorder. Part of Michael didn't want to care—after all, it was none of his business—but it was possibly at the heart of the issue.

Benedict wiped his face clean, his eyes and cheeks a

bright, plump red.

"I didn't... I didn't have a *choice*," he muttered as Aron continued to comfort him.

Michael did a double-take. What was that supposed to mean?

But then, Benedict looked to Michael with a haunting, disturbed stare that told him all he needed to know.

In an instant, he understood what they were dealing with.

"You were jealous of him," Michael said, recalling David's recounting of the torture story.

Benedict nodded, wiping his face with his forearm. "But that wasn't... that wasn't why I did what I did."

Everyone looked to him now. Aron dropped his hand to his side, but he remained the closest to Benedict.

"When I inherited DenCom..." The rest of the statement was visibly hard for him to continue. "... I was afraid. More afraid than I've ever been in my life. I didn't want to do it. I just wanted to take a desk job and try to have a normal life. All the Sasquatch and ghost hunts, that should've all stayed in the past. But Morecraft thought he saw something in me, something that could... that could handle harsh truth. I wish I knew what it was so I could just rip it out of me and..." He hesitated. "Morecraft wanted me to focus on finding something for a... well, all he called him was a *friend*. This friend wanted to know about an event that he claimed took place within the last two hundred years. He said that if it were true, it would prove to be one of the most paramount religious revelations in recent history."

"Who was it? The man who asked?"

Benedict nearly went into another tantrum at Michael's question, but contained his outburst to a few short lurches as if he were about to vomit.

"I'm... I'm not allowed to tell you. I can't tell you, or..."

"How would he know?"

"What?" Benedict's voice was weak, frail.

"How would he know if you told us about him?"

"Trust me, he'd know."

Michael could feel the man's genuine discomfort, but it was Aron who spoke next.

"He's threatened you?"

Benedict shook his head. "I can't say that."

"But it's what you think?"

He gave the subtlest of nods.

"Did he...?" Michael started, but he wasn't sure if he wanted to feed the fire. He trusted Aron's judgment, that Benedict was being honest, but he'd also just seen Benedict break down over one meaningless word. Regardless, he had to ask: "Did he force you to torture Von Gord?"

Benedict's eyes widened.

"He did, didn't he?"

"I can't speak poorly about him," Benedict began, shaking his head. "He's been my advisor for years, pointed me—and, by default, you guys—in all the right directions, and without him, I'd be no closer to solving the puzzle Morecraft left me."

"So, you thought it was better to torture a man than go against your advisor?" Michael asked.

"I *thought* it would be easier for him to *replace* me than try to sway me."

Michael caught the not-so-hidden meaning in the words, but he didn't let up. "From what David said, you were pretty enthusiastic about it."

Before Benedict answered, Michael caught Aron's questionable gaze. It wasn't often he saw genuine anger in his best friend's eyes, but he could see it brewing. Michael knew what Aron was trying to tell him: He was digging too deep, being too harsh on someone who, in his opinion, needed a compassionate response. But Michael couldn't take it seriously.

"I will admit, I... I was *frustrated* with him," Benedict replied. "I'd spent months, even years searching... I'd lost friends to the cause, people I'd loved like family. Then, this guy, this self-entitled little bastard, he's had it all handed to him on a silver platter. But he wasn't like the others I've seen. No, he wasn't the least bit grateful."

"Meaning?" Michael asked.

"... In my investigations, I've come across some people who just seem to *get* it. They know what it all means, know what... what the Valley was, what happened. Even if they didn't know, they *knew*. They just knew exactly what I'd sacrificed so much to even comprehend, and with less than a tenth of the effort. And there was no clear reason why."

"Are you saying there were others?" Michael asked.

"Others like Von Gord?"

"No, no!" Benedict replied. "They never called for what Von Gord did, and I was never ordered to ... do what I did to him again. Some of them understood and kept it quiet, usually after a visit from... Well, you know who I mean."

"But he made you deal with Von Gord yourself?"

Benedict nodded. "Don't bother asking why. I never learned myself."

"Did you ask?"

"I didn't *dare*. And if I were you, I wouldn't ask about his motives, either."

Michael went over Benedict's last statement again and again in his mind. Was it a warning or a threat? For the moment, though, he let it go in favor of furthering the conversation.

"All right, I won't," Michael said. "But what *can* you tell us?"

Benedict took in a long breath, choosing his words carefully. "Your investigations," he slowly replied, "have helped me and my advisor better understand what he and Morecraft wanted to know. We know that something did... *happen*. We found artifacts, mostly from an unnamed Native American tribe who we believe witnessed the event itself."

"The battle?" Michael asked.

Benedict gave a careful nod.

"Where did this happen?" Andrea asked.

"We believe it... it took place mostly in the Owens

Valley of California. We can't be sure yet, but that's where we've found what little physical evidence there is."

Michael knew the Valley well. It was bordered to the west by the Eastern Sierra Nevada mountains where Benedict had been lost for some time. He considered asking if there was any connection, but he chose to take the questions slowly, not wanting to get Benedict off track.

"Did *we* find any of that evidence?" Michael asked.

"The honest answer is: I don't know. There's never been enough to prove a connection. Most of the relics, I handled myself—what few there've been, anyway—but you've tried. The Antarctica investigation was the only one directly related to the events of the Valley thus far, simply because it was the best lead I had. Everything else you guys looked into was either a secondary interest, a possible relation, or just a hunch I acted on. Not all the investigations have ties."

"So, you really don't know more than Morecraft?" Michael asked.

"Not much, but some."

"Like what? If *this* is what we've been nearly killed over, we deserve to know."

"I can't tell you."

Michael's anger returned, but he tried not to show it. This was what he'd been afraid of: Benedict's resistance when it mattered most. He needed to know. He needed to understand what about this whole "Valley" thing was worth killing innocent people over.

Slowly, Michael reached around to his back pocket.

His fingers found the butt of the small gun—the last defense he had, should Benedict not go along with what he had to do. He had to *force* Benedict to answer the question. Then, he would deliver Benedict to the brothers, and—

No.

The thought came subtly, then proceeded to consume Michael's anger. His hand loosened around the gun.

No, Michael, not now. Not over this.

He felt his hand involuntarily leave the gun, and for a moment, he fought it, knowing the act was against his own will, like he'd somehow been possessed. But the thought immediately vanished, leaving only the acceptance that Benedict could not answer the question, and that was all he needed to know. He reached to adjust his suddenly ringing hearing aid.

"Thank ya, Michael."

"What?" Michael asked aloud, convinced he'd just heard one of them speak in a sing-song voice, calming yet taunting at the same time. He'd heard it clearly, as if the voice had been right next to him, the soft Texan accent unmistakable.

"I said, I can't tell you that," Benedict repeated.

Michael looked around the room for clarification. Everyone stared curiously back at him. He sighed; it must have been a glitch with the aid.

"I'll take that answer for now, Benedict," Michael said, "but someday, for all that's happened to us, all the danger we've been in, we'll want the truth. I can accept that it'll take time, but we will *not* be left out. I know how much you pay us to keep quiet, but if we're risking our lives for this, we deserve to know more. Know *everything*. Do you understand?"

Benedict slowly nodded. "All right. If it clears things up for now, and we can all be friends again, I promise that the moment I'm able to say something, I will."

"Okay. Now, there's one last thing I need to know before I decide how we're going to handle Von Gord," Michael said. "And I expect an *actual* answer from this."

Benedict nodded.

"Why did you choose us?"

Benedict frowned. "I'm sorry?"

"Think about it. None of us have any real experience relating to what you ask us to do. So why us? Why not hire people who actually know what they're doing, or who could do more?" Michael asked.

"Because I need all of you," he replied. "You all have a reason to be here, and you were carefully selected—or, in some cases, outright *named*—by my advisor as the only person suitable for the job."

"And what exactly *is* that job?" Michael asked. "Because I honestly feel like the only reason you keep us around is to have us run your errands and do weirdly mundane research. I understand if you want help, but the last thing you had me do was visit Western museums and write a twenty-page report on the Colt Dragoon. And when I asked why you chose me, you said it was because you noticed I hung decorative weapons on my wall. You of all people should know that that hardly makes me an expert."

"True, but I needed to see the facts in your own words."

"My *own* words?" Michael retorted, his anger gradually returning. "Benedict, you could've Googled everything you needed to know, even during most of our field work. And I know what you're going to say next: You can't be too careful, you need the information to come from a trusted source, what have you. But here's the reality: You refuse to handle even the *simplest* tasks on your own, but you're so damn *paranoid* that even within your own company, only a select few trusted people can wipe your ass, much less know the truth about you and the motives behind your investigations. Hell, it's been seven *years*, and you've never even told us your last name! So who can't you trust? The world around you, or yourself?"

"Michael, I've been... I've been embarrassed enough for one day. Can we please—?"

"No, Benedict." Michael could feel the internal fight to keep him calm, that ethereal force insisting that everything was going to be alright. But this wasn't just some conspiracy nonsense, anymore. This was his *life*. "If you can't tell us anything else, tell us this: Why us? Why are *we* so important to your investigations?"

"Because I need you all, okay? I can't say why. In some cases, I don't even know why, but you are all *essential* to my work. I'm telling you everything I can, really! I can't explain it, not because I don't *want* to, but because it *hurts*! I can't say it! I can't break the trust I've formed with you."

"Why, Benedict?"

"Because I need to keep you safe!"

"From who?"

"*From me!*"

Michael was speechless.

Everyone was speechless.

David had said that Benedict was a threat, but only if they prodded for more information and tried to force it out of him. But they'd already done exactly what David had said not to do. So what was Benedict going on about?

After a nearly a minute of thick, palpable silence, Benedict continued, "I know this is going to sound... *impractical*, but you are all by my side to keep you safe from anything I might have to do."

"What do you mean? Why would that keep us safe?" Michael asked.

Benedict swallowed. "In the future, for the sake of the Valley or otherwise, I might be called upon to do... certain things that could be harmful to you, if you're not by my side."

Michael raised an eyebrow.

"Listen, I can't tell you exactly for what, but we have to be ready. The next threat—the next *war*—will see DenCom in the spotlight, I can guarantee you that. And because of DenCom, future wars will never be fought the same way again. From advanced software to aircraft design, DenCom is leading the next technological renaissance, and all of us will play a part in it, not because we *want* to, but because we *have* to."

"Okay, I'm totally lost," Michael said.

"You should be," Benedict replied.

"But what would you have to do that could put us in danger?" Aron asked.

"That you haven't already done," Michael muttered.

Benedict hesitated. "I don't know, but I do know that, based on what my advisor has said, there's a lot coming our way. He wanted you involved, wanted you by my side to help me, and he also wanted to keep you out of the line of fire."

"Well, he's done a *great* job of that, hasn't he?" Michael asked.

"Well, even he would be able to admit that there's things we didn't account for," Benedict replied. "For instance, I thought Von Gord had died years ago. How he and his sons got this far, I still don't understand…"

Now, it was Michael's turn to reveal the dangerous secret. "David told me that after you stopped sending Von Gord supplies, a group from Russia came in and gave him everything he and his sons needed."

Benedict's face grew pallid. "Russia?"

"That's what David said," Michael replied. "Whoever they are, they're the ones supporting Von Gord and the brothers' efforts. Care to explain that one?"

"Just going by what you said… They're a small organization that may or may not be plotting to overthrow the Russian government. DenCom's been assisting the Russian authorities in their apprehension, but nothing's come as of recently."

"And in that, their goals align with Von Gord's," Michael said, remembering David's speech. "They want DenCom out of the way, too."

"I'd assume so, yes. I don't think they'd knock having someone who knows his way around a command line on their side, either."

"And three U.S.-trained soldiers," Michael added.

Benedict nodded.

"Well that solves that," Aron said. "I think we've got what we need."

It was clear Aron wanted this done and over with, as they all did, but Michael still wasn't done yet.

"Just to make sure I understand you correctly," Michael began, "you're trying to keep us safe from a variety of threats and from people who think we have some kind of connection to the events of the Valley. But all these crazy, drastic security measures were your advisor's idea, and he's forcing you to carry them out. You actually know a lot about what the Valley is and what it means, but you're just not allowed to say anything because it could literally change the world. And, just as an extra precaution, your advisor will make sure you take any action necessary to keep us, and this secret, safe. Did I hear all that correctly?"

"Yeah," Benedict panted. He looked in desperate need of a rest.

But he wouldn't get one. Not yet.

"Benedict?" Michael got the man's attention again, shakily standing up as he spoke. He confidently issued a command that he knew made him look just as crazy as Benedict.

But just barely.

"Call the *Bluestream*. Have it ready for departure tomorrow morning by six. We're going to Greenland."

35

IT WAS MIDNIGHT, AND DAVID WAS GROWING ANXIOUS.

The deadline was approaching, and he was worried that Michael had found an out. David wished they could have bugged or staked out the house, but the very most he felt comfortable doing was having Evans do a single drive-by, where he'd confirmed that there was a police car near the end of the condo's parking lot. While David had expected that much, he still took it as a sign that Michael might back out.

Since the tram crash, the brothers had been completely on their own: They hadn't heard anything else from their father, even after updating him on Michael. David wanted to think he was silently grieving for Erickson, but he didn't want to get his hopes up.

No authorities had bothered them, since the search in the mountains had taken most of their attention. The media's best guess was that they had possibly fled to Mexico. And apart from people jumping at anyone who vaguely resembled them, all had been quiet.

David looked over at the empty bed beside him as he sat in the same broken reading chair. They'd buried Erickson the night after the tram attack. David had tried to put it off, at least until Benedict was secured, but they knew that if they waited any longer, they would risk their brother's scent wafting into nearby rooms. When night came and the motel was quiet, they wrapped Erickson in one of the musty blankets and drove him into the desert. At the side of an unnamed, silent back road, they buried him with a pair of shovels they had found in the back of the Jeep. It was a sloppy, shallow grave, but one that wouldn't likely be disturbed. In truth, neither David nor Evans could remember where Erickson had been buried, except that it had a beautiful view of the clear night sky, and that a thorny barrel cactus would serve as his tombstone. Neither of them had spoken during their makeshift funeral service, and they had barely spoken since.

Now, it was a waiting game. They'd assumed their father would call again to tell them that the *Bluestream* had arrived in Palm Springs, but the phone hadn't rung once.

It finally did, just after twelve-thirty.

"Is this David?" Michael's strained voice came through the other line.

David hesitated at first. It wasn't the call they'd expected to come first, but it was still a pleasant surprise. "Yes. How's our situation?"

"I have Benedict with me, and he says your story's

true. He was late; apparently, traffic at Palm Springs International had caused a change in flight plan."

David didn't question it. So long as Michael had him, that was all that mattered. "Good. When can we go?"

"The airport's shut down for the night. Soonest we can leave is about six AM."

David tried not to be upset by this, knowing it was out of their control. "All right, where do we meet you?"

Michael gave him the address to the hangar. Although the small airport wasn't exactly quiet, it would most likely be deserted that early in the morning.

"All right. Call off the security at your house so they don't question where you're going," David ordered as he jotted down the meeting spot on a legal pad.

"Will do."

"Any security checkpoints?"

"I don't believe so. It's part of the civilian section, so just say you're with the DenCom flight and you should be good. But just so you're aware, I'll be armed for my own safety and so that Benedict won't be tempted to try anything. Is that all right with you?"

David thought about it carefully. No, it *wasn't* all right, not by a long shot. Would he be giving Michael too much trust, or was it a logical request? Reluctantly, David agreed that Michael could be armed, and they agreed to meet at six before hanging up.

36

Monday, July 29th
Ramone Estados Condo Complex
Palm Springs, California
5:31 AM

MICHAEL DIDN'T SLEEP THAT NIGHT, NOR DID ANYONE ELSE.

It had been a hard departure for everyone earlier that morning, brave faces being difficult to maintain with the weight they all carried. But they hoped to see each other again once this was over.

At Michael's request, Aron and Andrea had booked an early morning flight to Denver out of John Wayne Airport in Anaheim. Although the airport was a couple hours away, they couldn't risk leaving from Palm Springs and being seen by the brothers. The distraught pair had left at two AM to catch the first flight out at five, but not before Benedict had given them specific instructions on what to do once they reached DenCom Tower.

Michael and the nearly catatonic husk of Benedict found themselves alone for the remainder of the night. The hours went by slowly, awkward conversations about the plan for when they got to Greenland dotting the wait as Michael spent the majority of the time making arrangements for Granger.

He had no idea what would be left of their small group after this. In Greenland, Michael would stick with Benedict while acting the part of betrayer, but it was a role that came more naturally than he would've liked to admit. He was still upset, even furious that Benedict's "cover-your-eyes-and-it-disappears" mindset had almost led to their deaths on the Skyway Tram. However, the fact that Benedict was willing to face Von Gord told Michael he was at least capable of owning up to his mistakes. Before Aron and Andrea left, they had promised Benedict that if he went through with this, they would all stay with him and give him a clean slate.

Michael, on the other hand, hadn't made such an offer. Would he be able to truly forgive Benedict?

The only way to find out would be to survive.

When Michael told Benedict it was time to go, the man's life immediately returned to him, and he suddenly looked ready to face anything, come Hell or high water.

They left just after five-thirty, Michael leaving a key under the welcome mat for the zoo assistant he had called to take care of Granger. All he'd told the zoo was that he had a family emergency that required him to leave town the next morning, which apparently was enough.

Michael and Benedict headed to the car as the purples and oranges of sunrise gradated along the horizon. The cool of the night had yet to wear off, its chill nipping at Michael while Benedict was protected by his coat. A gentle breeze rocked the Birds of Paradise flowers on the path that led from Michael's condo to the parking lot.

They reached the Pantera. Michael got in first and unlocked the passenger door for Benedict, who stepped in with an unsettling smile and a spark in his eye. Michael's stomach turned; he had known Benedict long enough to know exactly what was going on in the man's distorted mind.

Benedict had chosen to consume his fear like a snake, letting irrationality swallow it whole for the time being. Fear would do nothing to help them; fear couldn't stop a bullet rushing toward their heads.

While insanity—the kind Benedict was capable of unleashing—could end lives.

"You ready?" Michael asked as he buckled himself in.

Benedict followed suit, slamming his buckle into place. "Oh, yes," he snarled with a cheeky grin.

As the car's engine roared to life, Michael pulled out of the parking lot overhang and headed toward the rising sun.

37

JUST AS THE SUN ROSE, ARON AND ANDREA MADE IT TO THE AIRPORT WITH AN HOUR TO SPARE. They checked in, went through security, and since neither of them had eaten since before Benedict's visit, they forced themselves to have a quick breakfast before boarding began.

Having to fly commercial again would be a strange experience for both of them. They always flew on the *Bluestream* if it was available, one of the many perks of working for the enigma that was DenCom. Now, with their future uncertain and the *Bluestream* in use, they found themselves waiting to board a large, unfamiliar aircraft jam-packed with people they didn't know. They would take their seats in first class and ignore the thought that their two best friends could be dead by nightfall.

They would land at Denver International, where a driver would be waiting to pick them up and take them to their first stop, DenCom Tower. After they did what they needed to do there, the two of them had agreed to split a hotel room in the greater Denver area, somewhere close to DenCom Tower in case they were needed again. And they were both desperate for the company, as they had proven to each other over the past week.

A spark had been ignited in their friendship, one that only they had noticed so far. Although they had been friends for years, the tram car crash changed things.

While she waited for Michael to come around or for Benedict to contact her, Andrea found herself visiting Aron often.

The first day they spent together had begun awkwardly enough. Both had been used to their conversations being offset by work, so they weren't accustomed to being able to talk for long periods of time. They couldn't remember the last time they'd had time to sit down and talk with each other—at least, outside of work or dinners with friends. However, over the course of Aron's hospital stay, things grew less awkward as they watched terrible daytime television, cracking jokes and riffing the subpar dramas that were all they had to watch.

As the day ended, Andrea mentioned how she had slept on their couch the previous night while watching Granger, since both her owners were out of commission. Feeding and watering the cat had led to a brief rest on the couch, with Granger soon joining her. Before she knew it, she and the cat had slept the night away.

Aron insisted that, if she planned on staying with Granger, she should get a good night's sleep on an actual bed, and he offered her his. Initially, she had not wanted to disturb their rooms, but Aron assured her several times it would not be an issue. If they were going to handle this right, they needed all the energy they could get. Reluctantly, she agreed to use his room for the night and not only woke up feeling much better, she also woke up with a new understanding of Aron and his interests, since they were plastered all over his wall.

Aron's interest in the Gothic genre didn't clash as much with Andrea's classic rock tastes as she thought they would. He had explained to her that while he had been a "casual goth" in high school, the musical and artistic tastes had remained into adulthood. They had spent the last several days discussing all the new movies, music, and books that Andrea had been introduced to and wanted to know more about.

But now, as their plane began to board, they were running out of conversation topics. They found themselves repeating things, talking about the same facts and bands over and over before the conversation dissolved into awkward silence. Yet as the reality of the situation set in, they knew it wasn't just their concern for Michael and Benedict's safety that they were covering up.

It was fear. Fear that began with their concerns but opened the door to something they knew was more than just friendship.

It hit both of them for the first time halfway through their flight, after the filler conversations had ended. Andrea chose to read a book for the last hour and a half of the trip, and Aron plugged himself into his music. Although neither knew, they were both having the same thought:

Son of a bitch, this better not be...

They forced the reality away, knowing it would only hinder their ability to think clearly, not to mention distort their vision of themselves as fearless, supportive friends. This couldn't get in the way. Perhaps, if there was an end in sight, they could revisit the idea.

But not now. Not yet.

So, for the time being, they let it go.

38

Monday, July 29th
Palm Springs International Airport
Palm Springs, California
6:05 AM

MICHAEL AND BENEDICT MADE IT TO THE MEETING PLACE ON TIME, THE BROTHERS HAVING YET TO ARRIVE.

The two pilots were waiting outside the hangar, looking sharp and ready as always. Benedict greeted them and gave them the basics, saying their guests would provide more specific information on where they were going. Without asking questions (they were no doubt used to this sort of thing from Benedict), the pilots headed back to the plane to ready for departure.

Less than five minutes later, a beat-up Jeep rounded the corner of the lot. Michael recognized David, who had yet to change his hair color back and shave, in the driver's seat. The car quickly pulled in alongside the Pantera. David and who Michael assumed was one of his brothers exited with their guns holstered.

They looked Benedict up and down, their glare clearly meant to intimidate, but Benedict held himself together, staring blankly back into his soon-to-be kidnapper's rough face.

"Wait a minute..." Benedict said as he closely examined each of the men, then turned to Michael, jerking his thumb over his shoulder at the brothers. "Weren't there three of these assclowns?"

The unnamed brother rushed forward and punched Benedict square in the nose. He stumbled but didn't fall.

"Evans!" David shouted.

"What?" Evans replied. "It's not like Father won't do worse!"

"Ooh, sounds like fun!" Benedict's voice was nasally, as he used both hands to stop his nose from gushing blood. "Can I bring my whip? Or would the diamond studs be too flashy for you boys?"

Michael tried to remain stoic, but he could see right through Benedict's act. He was frightened—incredibly frightened—using humor to distract himself from the gravity of the situation.

David sighed. "Search him."

As Evans began to search through Benedict's pockets and coat, David turned to Michael. "Where are the pilots?"

Michael filled David in, his explanation coming to an end just as they heard Benedict give a small shout. They looked over to see the long, black coat pulled to the side and Evans's right hand in Benedict's back pocket.

"Save it for after dinner, you pervert!"

Evans retrieved his hand, staring daggers into the smaller man. He looked ready to flatten Benedict when David stopped him.

"Cut the crap, both of you!" He focused on Evans.

"Anything?"

Evans shook his head.

David approached Benedict, who made no effort to back down. He grasped the pendant and ripped it from Benedict's neck, the metal chain audibly snapping. Benedict grunted, then reached up to rub the back of his neck where a visible red ring began to grow. If Benedict had a snappy retort, he kept it to himself, which Michael was grateful for.

David placed the pendant in his shirt pocket, then turned his attention back to Michael. "Let's go."

Michael nodded as he headed for the plane, ready to force Benedict ahead of him if, for some reason, he decided to put up a fight.

They got inside and began to settle as David knocked on the cockpit door. When one of the pilots stepped out, David handed the man a sheet of paper. After looking it over, Michael heard him say that the trip was possible, but it would require at least one fuel stop. David agreed, but Michael could see that he was visibly annoyed that the flight would not be direct.

"All right, here's the deal," David began as he got comfortable on one of the two couches at the front of the plane. "Benedict, you will not utter a *word* unless spoken to. You will not move unless given permission, and you will not give us any trouble. I know firing a shot in this thing would be a death sentence, but I'll do what I have to. Is that understood?"

"Sure, Mom," Benedict drawled, causing David's glare

to harden.

"Don't test me." He lay back on the couch next to Evans, then turned to him. "I'll keep watch. You rest."

Evans obliged, falling asleep as they reached the runway.

During the majority of the trip, Benedict remained silent. Michael knew why: He wanted to save his best insults for when he finally came face to face with Von Gord.

39

Aron and Andrea landed in Denver at ten-thirty that morning, catching their first glimpse of DenCom Tower as they made the final approach. Although they were still a fair distance from the city, DenCom Tower stood out along the horizon as the tallest skyscraper by at least a third.

After landing, the pair quickly got off the plane and raced to meet with the driver, whom they found standing at the base of the escalator leading to baggage claim. Having only brought carry-on bags for what they hoped would be a short stay, they were taken straight to the car and got comfortable for yet another short ride.

The drive to DenCom Tower was plagued by late morning traffic, which would have doubled their commute time if it hadn't been for Benedict's choice of private driver.

Aron and Andrea had been used to the older, butler-type chauffeur whom Benedict always kept on standby in California. However, this one, who had introduced himself as Louis (although he made a point to say he preferred being called Loose), was much younger and much more impatient than Benedict's usual driver. Once in the city, he expertly navigated the twisting and turning roads at seemingly triple-digit speeds, pulling tricks and maneuvers that gave Aron flashbacks (and Andrea a better understanding) of the tram crash. They feared they would get pulled over—and, at one point, they nearly did.

Halfway to Denver, a city officer on a motorcycle had turned on his sirens and raced for the car. As he drew closer, however, Aron and Andrea saw him look down at the car's license plate. His blinkers went off almost immediately, and as he fell back into traffic, he gave Loose a friendly wave, which he returned to the rearview mirror with a grin.

Denver was Benedict's town, inside and out, even if the public didn't know it. Neither Aron nor Andrea had been to the city in years, and they had forgotten the kind of influence the man—or, rather, the company—had. Being the single most lucrative business in Denver, DenCom and its CEO had given plenty of money back to the city, supporting homeless and women's shelters as well as local charities and artistic ventures, so DenCom was allowed to skirt a few light rules here or there. Local politicians and government officials had high regard for DenCom's goodwill work, and it didn't go unnoticed that they brought massive business to the city. If Benedict had asked for other special privileges in return, Aron and Andrea didn't know. The only one they did know of was the name change of the street that led to DenCom Tower, now called Benedict Street. On their last trip, they had asked him about the name change.

"Well, I just liked the thought of people in town sayin' stuff like, 'If ya wanna get anywhere in Denver, ya gotta go down on Benedict.'"

As they finally reached the city and found their way onto Benedict Street, DenCom Tower's silver facade shone like a beacon in the midday sun. The tower was an odd design: The top portion was the standard rectangular shape, and was often compared in passing to the original World Trade Center. Yet two other sections came up from the base, ascending to roughly halfway up the main building and tapering off at angles, the left side rising higher than the right.

It was the staple of the city, the building every tourist caught in pictures but was never sure exactly what it was. The bold, white capital letters spelling *DENCOM* on the building's front and back gave it away, but few people bothered to find out what it meant.

Loose pulled up to DenCom Tower in an illegal maneuver that was met with a chorus of horn blares. After Aron and Andrea thanked him, he drove off to their hotel where he would check them in and drop off their bags.

The building's glass exterior gave Aron and Andrea a clear view of their path. They hurried into the building up three sets of cement stairs as dozens of businessmen and women passed them, oblivious to their presence.

They did exactly as Benedict had instructed, bypassing the reception area and heading straight for the elevator. Aron pressed the button that would take them to the thirtieth floor of the hundred-and-five-story building. From there, they had little trouble finding the room they were looking for.

The floor appeared deserted, with not so much as a janitor lazily mopping the halls. Directly in front of them as they exited the elevator was a jet-black door, adorned by a single label painted in white:

NETWORKING HUB 17: ADVANCED PRACTICE

Few people in the company knew what—or *who*—it was. Aron and Andrea were to be the newest inductees to the secret, and neither of them had a clue what to expect as the door slid open on its own.

Before them was a clearly lit path like that of a movie theater or an aircraft aisle, lined with small, white LED lights that stretched into the darkness. At the end of the short path, although hard to make out, was what appeared to be a free-floating television screen buzzing with static.

Andrea was the first to enter the room, unfazed by the odd surroundings. She had been on movie sets and the like for years, so she was used to the strange atmosphere. Aron, however, was obviously skittish; he remained visibly calm, but he couldn't keep himself from yelping as the door slid shut behind them.

As Aron looked back to Andrea, she chuckled and rolled her eyes.

"My hero," she sighed.

Before Aron could come up with a witty comeback,

an image began to form in the mirage of static on the screen. A long, bald head appeared, almost bending the static around it to create a three-dimensional picture.

"Are you with Benedict?" a small, distorted voice asked.

"Yes," Andrea said as they reached the end of the path, Aron tensing behind her.

"Are you here to frame the picture, or take the call?"

"The call," Andrea replied, recalling Benedict's instructions.

"Aya, and the password?"

"F you Michael." Again, as Benedict had instructed. Although paraphrased, she hoped the strange man would take it.

"Well, I suppose it's close enough," he said as all the lights in the room glowed to life at once.

A swarm of monolithic supercomputers and mainframe servers came into view, the room filled with the humming of what had to be hundreds of booting machines.

Beyond them, as the static-filled screen rose to the ceiling, Aron and Andrea made out a raised cement platform. Sitting atop it was a large maple desk, where the man from the screen casually sat. Behind him, even more black desks sat along a wall of what had to be at least fifty monitors. The man stood up, proving to be taller than either of them had thought possible for a human being, and cheerily waved to the pair.

They reached one of the two cement stairways that

led to the platform where they were greeted by the tallest, palest, and skinniest man they had ever met. At nearly seven feet tall, his skin was paper white. His face was dull but inviting, and his immaculately polished bald head perfectly reflected the ceiling lights and monitors around him. As the strange man threw his arms open in greeting, Aron and Andrea had to fight to contain their questions.

"Welcome to Networking Hub 17. Has Benedict told you what goes on here?" the man asked. There was little difference between his filtered and unfiltered voice, as it was still unusually high-pitched, monotone, and somewhat nasally. Even in person, there appeared to be some level of distortion in his speech. They shook their heads. While they had both visited DenCom Tower before, they had never been granted access to—or even been told about—Networking Hub 17 until now. All Benedict had given them were the instructions about how to get in.

"Well, to start, you can call me Nelson. I believe you and I have already spoken," he said to Andrea, who quickly recalled where she had heard his voice before.

"You were the guy who called me about the tram crash! How did you know what happened so quickly?" she asked.

"Benedict has a chip in his body," Nelson explained. "He had it surgically implanted in case of an emergency, much like the one he was just in. It monitors his life signs and alerts me of any significant change in his vitals."

"A chip?" Aron said, visibly surprised. "I would've thought he'd hate the idea."

"There's a lot you two don't know about him, and hopefully, that will help us today," Nelson replied.

"What exactly are we doing?" Andrea asked.

"Well, to start, the chip also allows us to track his every move, so we'll know exactly where they're taking him." Nelson stepped aside and motioned to a pair of chairs near the monitors. "From here, we'll have everything we need to make this operation a success and get both Michael and Benedict out of there safely, so I suggest we have a seat and wait for them to land."

The pair obliged and headed for the chairs.

"Getting them out is the most important thing, but what about the files on Benedict's flash drive? Are we just going to let those go?" Aron asked.

Nelson smirked. "What files?"

40

THE *BLUESTREAM* HAD JUST PASSED THE BORDER INTO GREENLAND AND WAS HEADING TOWARD THE DISTANT MOUNTAINS. Below, the land was already dark, night having met them quickly as they flew east.

Over the intercom, the pilots announced that they'd made contact with a man who was guiding them onto the small airstrip. It would still be a half hour or so before they could land, but the process was well underway.

Michael stared out the window in the back of the plane, watching the green landscape slowly shift into icy tundra. He had watched state after state, country after country pass beneath them, the usual pleasantries of the private jet unavailable by order of David. So Michael had watched, fighting the urge to give into sleep, as he knew Benedict had.

His sides and back still ached from what had been the longest seven days of his life. However, the pain was far from his primary concern. The most pressing issue, aside from their desperate plan, was his growing exhaustion.

He hadn't slept in nearly twenty hours.

Or had it been twenty-four?

He couldn't be certain, but he knew he was tired, and on more than one occasion, he had considered taking a nap. But he didn't want to take the chance that the brothers would drag Benedict off without him.

Instead, he worried about where this morally-confused justice would lead all three parties. Although he knew that the end result could be his and Benedict's deaths, he tried to ignore that possibility; it would serve no good purpose.

Michael had always believed that when his time to die came, there would be no out, no trick to escape death's talons. He would fight, but he wouldn't run. If this happened to be the end for him, even if it wasn't by his design, he would face it with courage.

Still, that didn't mean he wasn't tempted to run.

Michael knew that Benedict was far from ready to die. The last few days had shown him the depths of Benedict's tunnel vision, which he hoped wouldn't affect them as they carried out their mission.

For the moment, he looked like he could hold it together, but when it came time to address his actions, would he be so noble?

Michael feared the answer was no.

41

VON GORD, A NIGHT OWL BY NECESSITY, COULD SEE THE DIM LANDING LIGHTS OF DENCOM'S PRIVATE JET ON FINAL APPROACH. The subpar airstrip was lit for the first time in weeks, coating the surrounding forest in reds, greens, and blues. And, as always, the longer he looked outside, the more irritated he became.

His naked, unblinking eyes were burning.

The exposed organs were more comfortable in the darkness, and even when they did become strained, the nerve suppressors blocked out most of the pain and discomfort. But, like his sons, his weekly injections were due. He would tend to them after disposing of Benedict.

But at the moment, even the monitors were hard to look at. He focused on the green monitor again, as he had the past hour, and watched the plane come in on the radar screen. The screeching of tires and engines in the distance accompanied the green blip in front of him.

The image comforted Von Gord, knowing that Benedict was finally here, that he would pay for what he had done so many years ago. The thought engrossed him as the plane rolled down the runway, distracting him from the rotting corpse of a cowboy who stood behind him, breathing down his neck.

Yet, since his condition limited nearly all basic senses, such mundane things often went unnoticed.

Once he knew they were on the ground and getting ready to enter the house, he would retreat to his room. When Benedict and his betrayer came upstairs, he would join them while Benedict watched his dreams die.

As he heard the plane's engines power down, Von Gord turned his wheelchair toward the hallway leading to the darkness of his bedroom. He hated the thing, hated the creaking and groaning it made whenever it moved. He hated the fact that he had to rely on others for nearly everything, even simple tasks that, in another life, he would have taken for granted. He hated the fact that although he was no young man, he felt far older than he was.

He hated that, if it hadn't been for the drugs, every move he made would have caused pain. He hated his frail and flaky skin that periodically fell off in patches, then grew back in a seemingly endless cycle. He hated that he couldn't do such mundane tasks as make himself food, that he was limited to what those idiot Russian guards knew how to make him. He hated that, while he had his sons' help, he still felt alone.

But even more, he hated Benedict.

With all the fires of that damned Valley, he hated Benedict.

42

THE *BLUESTREAM* WAS A LARGE PLANE, BUT IT WASN'T BIG ENOUGH TO REQUIRE A LADDER TO EXIT. The door folded down into a stairway, and Michael stepped out first, followed by Benedict, David, and Evans.

They were led through a gated entrance to a short pathway. The ground and sparse plants were dark and wet, as if it had rained recently. The humidity was thick and stifling, far removed from the dry desert air of Southern California.

From the view on the flight in, Michael had expected an icy landscape and a simple shack with a small, dirt airstrip. But he couldn't have predicted what he was greeted with as he exited the plane.

The mansion looked oddly out of place, considering their current setting. Painted maroon red with black trimmings, it looked downright Gothic when set against the dark landscape. The house had three floors that extended high above the group, the second of which appearing to have a panoramic window where the only light shone through the gaps in the thick curtains shrouding it. To either side, the house extended into adjacent rooms and wings that likely continued farther back. And atop the house were several, high-rising spires adorned with statues of winged men ready to leap forward and strike. Water seemed to stream down from their oversized hollow eyes.

Surrounding the house was a black, wrought iron fence that only showed the tiniest hints of rust. Between the house and the fence was a large but clearly neglected garden. Most of the dying plants along the path were drenched, their leaves vainly hanging onto droplets that shimmered in the moonlight.

A forest surrounded them on all sides, broken only by the distant snow-capped mountains. Although not an ice field, the terrain was rugged and out of the way, so the whole setup perplexed Michael. The house was supposed to be Von Gord's grandfather's, but why have such a lavish mansion in such a remote location?

But Benedict appeared to be even more surprised than Michael, he noted when he saw his boss survey the area. He assumed Benedict knew the lay of the land, at least at the time of Von Gord's banishment. But Benedict kept looking around—from fear or curiosity, Michael wasn't sure. What he did know was that Benedict's eyes soon fell upon two skinny guards standing by the front door.

They stepped onto a large, creaky deck as David and Evans greeted the guards.

"How is he?" Evans asked.

"Content, sir," a guard replied, looking straight ahead as if he were being interrogated by a superior officer.

"Great, then he's pissed," David said.

Michael didn't pay attention as the brothers continued to discuss their plan with the guards. Instead, he watched Benedict, following his gaze to the right guard's shoulder patch.

Michael examined it himself, noting the hammer and sickle in the center of the black, round patch, the tools and trimming sewn in blood red. He didn't have enough time to contemplate the strange markings before being shown inside.

As the soldiers opened the large double doors, they entered a lavish foyer. The doors were soon shut behind them; the dim moonlight from a hexagonal window above the entrance now their only lighting. But surprisingly, it was enough to reveal the layout of the room.

The foyer was painted red with gold trimmings. In the corners, cobwebs grew in the darkness, creating a blurred veil over more of the winged men statues. A grand staircase leading up to the second floor, perhaps beyond, lay ahead of them. To their right, a hallway led deeper into the house. To their left, Michael saw a pair of golden elevator doors.

"Evans, lead them upstairs," David said as he headed for the elevator. "Father should be with you shortly."

"Oh, joy," Benedict muttered as they began their ascent.

43

NELSON WOKE ARON AND ANDREA AS THE *BLUESTREAM* TOUCHED DOWN. They had both fallen asleep hours before, much to Nelson's dismay. He finally had people to talk to, to share his knowledge with, but after hours of tedious questions, his new friends had needed rest. Nelson obliged and let them sleep nearby, still within reach in case the plane landed.

Nelson worked to get a better visual of the surrounding area at Benedict's location. All he had for the moment was a blurry image of the *Bluestream* at the end of a runway. To the plane's right was a house that appeared as a red-and-black blur in the dim moonlight. Further down the runway, Nelson could make out another gray smudge that he assumed was a small outbuilding.

As the image gained clarity, they could make out four figures against the lights of the plane and airstrip. This time, they could easily see who was who.

"Looks like they're heading inside," Nelson said as the image was replaced by one of the four people approaching the larger building, leaving the dim light of the *Bluestream*. Behind them, the plane appeared to be powering down, the lights inside captured mid-dim. The pilots would likely stay on the plane during the meeting, so Nelson wouldn't bother with them again.

"How long do you think it'll take?" Aron asked, a yawn following the question.

"Not more than five minutes," Nelson replied as both screens adjacent to the satellite view came to life. Various windows began to appear—some console applications spitting out numbers, some complex-looking charts and diagrams—all in preparation for the incoming data.

"Listen carefully. I'll need your help for some of this." Nelson motioned to the left monitor. "This is data from Benedict's sensor. It'll show if he's stressed or injured."

Aron and Andrea looked over at the monitor, which was growing more coherent as the program translated and began to display the data. Monitors for heart rate, breathing, and much more appeared on the screen. Neither Aron nor Andrea quite understood what they were seeing most of the time, but it was simple enough to tell from color coding that Benedict's blood pressure was slowly rising.

"Over here," Nelson continued as he motioned to the right monitor, "is a program that should route the feed into our system. With any luck, we'll be inside within a minute of receiving the signal."

Aron and Andrea hoped he was right. If there was any indication that Benedict's pendant was not a simple flash drive, Von Gord might kill him and Michael without a second thought.

The pendant was, indeed, a flash drive for his files, but it was also a backdoor device. At Benedict's request, Nelson had added the feature after they'd already received the finished pendant.

All of Benedict's classified files were indeed on the pendant, which he would tell any would-be kidnappers. However, as soon as they plugged the device into a computer, the backdoor would be silently activated, giving Nelson the ability to hack into nearly any system.

He would use the pendant to break into Von Gord's systems and take what information he could before their airstrike leveled the home.

The only challenge would be getting Michael and Benedict out safely. There were several options, from hacking into the mansion's security system and faking an alert, to engaging in a full-scale raid. Most of the options, however, did not guarantee their safety.

Their air support had been dispatched hours earlier, stealthily trailing the *Bluestream* to its final destination, undetectable by radar. Now, that same air support was sending updated pictures. Aron and Andrea had yet again asked for more details.

"Full disclosure has not been approved at this time," was all Nelson felt comfortable saying, albeit robotically. Even if he wanted to, he couldn't risk them knowing any more than they needed to. Not yet.

After saying this, he'd gone back to work. Aron and

Andrea stopped asking, though Nelson suspected they were coming to their own conclusions.

Once he was in Von Gord's system, the files would be sent directly to a secure drive on one of Nelson's supercomputers. All they could do for now was monitor Benedict's vital signs as they held steady.

44

Monday, July 29th
Greenland Compound
8:15 PM (Greenland Time)

MICHAEL, BENEDICT, AND EVANS WALKED UP THE REMAINDER OF THE GRAND STAIRCASE. Evans then directed them down the right hallway toward a faintly lit room at the end.

The room's dim lighting came from a set of six monitors, two levels of three, displaying four separate feeds per screen. Most showed the house or surrounding areas: Three of the feeds showed David searching through what appeared to be a small armory. Others showed various hallways and outdoor views. Over half the feeds were of the house, surrounding forests, the *Bluestream*, and even a view from an outbuilding they had seen during landing.

But the remaining feeds caught Michael by surprise.

At least six were from Benedict's personal security systems—at DenCom Tower *and* his own home. Four showed various levels of DenCom Tower: Two for the main entrance, one for the parking garage, and another for Benedict's office.

The last two showed what Michael knew to be Benedict's home, one feed showing his large, rustic living room, while the other showed the hallway leading to his bedroom.

If he had these cameras, what was to stop him from getting into the rest of the system?

What was to stop him from watching Nelson?

Michael saw the fear in Benedict's eyes, but he himself wasn't quite as stunned by the discovery. Although Michael had been filled in on Aron and Andrea's part of the plan, including how they were supposed to meet up with Nelson, he wasn't expecting it to work perfectly, given how everything else had gone so far. He knew he'd have to improvise, to draw on everything he'd learned during his time working for DenCom. He just hoped Benedict didn't screw it up.

Michael made out a small couch illuminated by the monitors. Like everything in the house, it was Victorian-style with blackened wood and red cushions. Behind that, he saw the curtains that blocked off the panoramic window he had seen from outside.

"Please sit down," a groggy voice spoke through the speakers on the monitors. *"I will be with you shortly."*

Michael and Benedict stared at each other. The voice had been unlike any they had heard today: It sounded old, weathered, and having the hoarseness of a long-time smoker. Reluctantly, the pair sat together on the couch, Benedict on the left side, Michael on the right.

Then, everything went black.

Benedict jumped as the darkness consumed them. Michael simply took it in stride, patiently waiting for whatever was to come.

Neither man could see an inch in front of his face.

The only sound they heard other than their own breathing was the monitors powering down, which was soon followed by two pairs of boots approaching from the hallway.

David's was among them. His gait sounded just as it had in the hospital halls.

The creaking of door hinges, slowly followed by the screeching of wheels, cut through Michael's thoughts. The sound grew closer, stopping just inches from Benedict, whom Michael felt quivering beside him as wheezing filled the air. The breath hit his face at the same time as the smell: like that of rotted meat. Both sensations were overpowering, but neither man made a move or sound.

The bulging thyroid eyes were the first thing Michael saw.

The orbs seemed to hover in place within the deep, maroon eye sockets.

The nose caught his attention next, like that of a skeleton but skinnier and more slit-like than wide. Michael could also see the lipless mouth and orange, shattered teeth as the monitors illuminated the room once again. His skin was white and wrinkled, the dark patches of melted flesh standing out in the growing light.

Benedict had jumped up, shock taking hold before he could scream. He only stared at the man, looking upon his work.

"Good to see you, old friend," Von Gord rasped, and

Benedict finally screamed.

Von Gord laughed as if for the first time in years.

45

VON GORD LOOKED TO MICHAEL, WHO HAD TO FIGHT AVOIDING THE HIDEOUS MAN'S GAZE. With what little face was left, Michael could tell the man was conveying a look of gratitude. If it was genuine or not, he couldn't tell.

There wasn't any hope of reading between the lines with this man. Both Michael and Benedict would have to act with caution; especially given what Benedict had already put him through, pushing this man too far could prove unwise.

"Thank you for bringing him to us," Von Gord said. "I'm glad you could see things from our family's perspective."

"Once I knew the truth, there was no debate." Michael let his gaze fall to David behind the wheelchair and Evans beside him, then to Benedict who'd just finished collecting himself. "I don't like being lied to."

Von Gord nodded slowly, then looked to his sons. "The drive."

David wheeled his father back to the monitors, an assault rifle now slung over his back. His hands flew across the expansive keyboard at inhumanly fast speeds as various windows appeared on the screens. The blocks of commands that scrolled across the screen were gibberish to Michael, but this man clearly knew what he was doing.

David retrieved the necklace from his shirt pocket and put it in his father's thin, outstretched hand. Grasping it tightly, Von Gord shifted around as he worked with the pendant, trying to find the hidden USB connector.

It wasn't long before he'd separated the pendant from the silver top that connected it to the chain. He held it up to the light like the trophy it was, then plugged it into one of towers beneath the desk.

Immediately, several new displays appeared on the screen. Although their meaning was unclear to Michael, they made Von Gord sigh.

"We're going to be here a while," he said.

The files themselves would have been a simple break, but the advanced decryption programs were moving at a snail's pace.

Just as Benedict had said they would.

By now, Nelson had to be hard at work, the files already safe back in DenCom's servers.

Yet any sense of accomplishment Michael felt was wiped away with Von Gord's next words.

"Let's kill some time," he said as Evans took over his father's wheelchair and wheeled him around. "While we wait, I might as well see what I can get from you."

David retrieved a long, black box from a nearby table on Benedict's side, opening it before showing its contents to their father. Von Gord let his hand fall on the handle of the small device, then looked up at David.

"Good choice, son."

The cattle prod let out a spark as Von Gord prepared

it. He neared Benedict, who drew farther back into his seat. His eyes were locked on the pointed prongs, like the fangs of some deadly serpent. Von Gord came to a slow stop, glaring at Benedict as he spoke.

"Don't worry, if I have my way, this will be far from the worst thing I'm going to do to you. And I *will* have my way."

Benedict didn't have time to react before the prongs were jammed into his neck. He convulsed, then fell limp.

Michael jumped to his feet, instinctively ready to defend Benedict, but caught himself before he could act.

Keep in character, he reminded himself. *Don't give yourself away.*

Benedict now had the loveseat to himself as the two brothers glared briefly at Michael. He worried that they would force him back down, but since their father had paid no mind to Michael, they let it go.

His eyes burning with pure hatred, Von Gord only pushed the prongs in deeper as Benedict continued to convulse. Michael could do nothing but watch as small patches of blood began to form where the prongs met Benedict's flesh.

46

Monday, July 29th
Networking Hub 17
Denver, Colorado
4:23 PM (Mountain Time)

NELSON SPRANG TO THE KEYBOARDS AS THE MONITORS ALERTED HIM OF BENEDICT'S SUFFERING.

He was working his way carefully through Von Gord's defenses, taking whatever information he could find that could prove useful. Benedict's files had been the first thing to go, along with slowing Von Gord's various decryption programs to buy them some time.

"It looks like they're tasering him," he said as his hands flew across the keyboard. "Whatever they're using, it's strong. If they don't let up, it could fry his chip!"

Andrea gasped as they watched Benedict's numbers spike. After thirty grueling seconds, the numbers dropped, but Benedict was still in severe pain, even danger.

Nelson sighed; they would be seeing alerts like that for a while.

Although Von Gord's systems were complex for the average hacker—or a seasoned one for that matter—Nelson saw it as nothing more than a child's placemat maze. But it would still take time to solve the puzzle and for Von Gord's computer to understand exactly what Nelson wanted upon gaining control of the system. Plus, this was still enemy territory, a digital warzone.

He had to be careful. Even the most minuscule misstep could tip Von Gord off to a breach in security. He had expected more resistance as he worked his way deeper into the system, but he hoped for minimal distractions.

Aron and Andrea watched, amazed as the strange man typed away at the keyboard. There was little they could do to help.

But Nelson knew they wanted to be there. They needed to see this through to the end.

47

VON GORD REMOVED THE PROD AND PUSHED HIMSELF AWAY FROM BENEDICT. No lasting damage had been done, but Benedict was winded and would need time to gather himself.

Von Gord would not allow it.

"What did I see?" he asked Benedict, leveling the prod at his chest. It was close enough that Benedict could feel the crackle of electricity in the air.

"No clue," he lied with one quick breath, and Von Gord jammed the prod into Benedict's chest.

Von Gord slouched back in his wheelchair, almost casually watching as Benedict reeled with pain.

Benedict was beginning to lose it. He was a mess. As the prod was removed, his body began involuntarily twitching, and his hair stood up in patches.

"Well, I guess we'll have to start with the lesser questions, then. Sound good?" Benedict didn't say a word, but his bloodshot eyes stared back at Von Gord with unhindered anger. "Glad you agree. So, who killed JFK?" Von Gord asked.

Benedict took in a long breath, then let his mind speak when his body urged him not to. "John Wilkes Booth, of course."

Von Gord growled as Benedict recited his disturbed, sarcastic piece, pausing as he erupted into the occasional coughing fit. "A group called... Majestic 12 brought him back... as a cyborg because he... he was the best at killing presidents..."

Von Gord roared as he thrust the prod beneath Benedict's chin in the very center of his jaw, causing another blood-curdling spasm.

Benedict had sarcastic answers for all of Von Gord's questions, most of which had likely been thought up on the plane ride. They were all for his own benefit, a mental trick to get him through the pain.

Over the course of the "torture session", Benedict gave Von Gord one insane cover story after another. "*Amelia Earhart had discovered Atlantis on her final flight, then lived her remaining days as Arthur Curry's mistress*" was the least offensive of them. The jokes were tasteless and meant to anger Von Gord, which they succeeded in doing. Benedict gave his final answer, and the prod was shoved into his right armpit. But through the pain, Benedict knew their plan was working. Von Gord had not looked at the monitors once since beginning the interrogation, which meant he hadn't noticed that his program had made little progress in actually decrypting the files.

He cursed at Benedict in frustration as he removed

the prod, then began a series of quick jabs to Benedict's chest and stomach. The voltage was near maximum. With each strike, Benedict shuddered and violently convulsed. He felt saliva involuntarily flowing from his mouth like a courtyard fountain.

"*Why! Wont! You! Talk!?*" Von Gord shouted between jabs, then leaned back in his wheelchair, seemingly defeated. The brothers tried to comfort their father, but he waved them away with a loud grunt.

Von Gord searched Benedict's eyes for some kind of middle ground, some unreachable understanding of what bound them and brought them together in the first place. He didn't know where they would end up.

But they both knew where it had all started.

48

Another Time.
Another Place.
Another Life.

ONCE, DURING HIS DAYS AT DENCOM, WILLIAM VON GORDON HAD BEEN A SMALL, WEAK, YET DETERMINED MAN. His life had been less than pleasant leading up to when he worked at DenCom, but he always made the most of it.

Things never seemed to go as planned, not even in his youth.

Early in his senior year of high school, Gordon, as he preferred being called then, had managed to get two girls pregnant within weeks of each other. The first, Abigail, the mother of the triplets, had been a kind-hearted girl who had fallen for him years earlier.

They had done it for the first time in the back of his old Honda, deep in the woods outside of Cleveland where they grew up. Back then, Gordon had been healthy and attractive, with thick-rimmed glasses hiding potential that only Abigail had seen.

The second girl had been a mistake.

Her name was Jasmine, a lunatic and notorious slut. She claimed having Gordon's child was the will of God, but she didn't tell him that part until, against his better judgment, he'd already done the deed. She announced her pregnancy in front of the whole school during lunch one day, standing atop a cafeteria table and screaming praise to her twisted image of God, thanking Him for the honor of bearing the true Immaculate Conception. The show effectively ended his relationship with Abigail, who only saw him again after the triplets were born.

Gordon adjusted to life as the part-time dad of three, only allowed to be a father when Abigail needed him. But only weeks after their birth, Jasmine called from her birthing room to deliver the message that: "The little bitch is here. Come get her."

Gordon rushed to the hospital and was met with pure and utter chaos. At the first opportunity she saw, Jasmine had shattered the window beside her bed and used the glass to cut her wrists, slicing down both arteries with surgical precision. There was a note by her side scribbled in blood, letting the world know that her job in this life was done.

He didn't have time to grieve, even if he wanted to. There were bigger issues to deal with.

In less than a month, he had become the father of three sons and one daughter. The daughter, having no other close family to care for her, was placed in Gordon's custody.

He'd already committed to Omaha for college, but the little girl that, in her suicide note, Jasmine had named Aral couldn't join him. He felt a strong attachment to her and didn't want to let her leave his life, especially since this was the only one of his children he had the opportunity to raise. But as money became tight and the move grew closer, Gordon knew that his only option was to give her up to a good home.

Even though Aral's adopted family let Gordon keep in touch with her as she grew older, it didn't make things any easier when he found himself so far away. Trying to juggle Aral, his three sons with Abigail, college, and his personal life, the stress had gradually eaten away at him.

It wasn't until he graduated from college that all of Gordon's children had been in a room together for the first time. They were just under five when Gordon had flown out and arranged the special get-together. Aral had taken to her new brothers nicely, and the triplets had become very protective of their half-sister. In the years to come, the two families had arranged several more play dates, especially when Abigail and her family had moved closer to where Aral's adopted family was living, which led to the triplets and their half-sister sharing a very close bond.

Meanwhile, Gordon had to watch from the sidelines as his children grew. Soon after graduating, he was hired by DenCom to work at the help desk, so he had to relocate to Denver and leave his children behind in Ohio yet again. Being in an entry-level position, he never had the money or time for more than one or two trips home a year for holidays.

But as the years went by and Gordon moved up in DenCom's IT hierarchy, he couldn't help but notice that

Aral was growing detached from the rest of her strange, separated family, even refusing to confide in her brothers, who she was said to have loved more than anyone else.

Then, there was the day she went to school and never came home.

Aral was barely fourteen when it happened. She and another child were declared missing. Heartbreaking theories were presented based on good evidence, but Gordon, as well as Aral's adopted parents, refused to believe she would do what the reports implied. But after the recent suicide of a neighborhood friend was cited, the authorities considered the case closed.

For Gordon, this was the beginning of the end. He knew inside that her probable suicide had been his fault. He hadn't been there enough. He hadn't been the father she needed.

He neglected his health to put money toward investigations to find her or, at the very least, a body. Years went by with no leads, and in those years, Gordon fell into a deep depression. Although he tried to move on, the past wouldn't let him.

As his sons graduated and tried to make their own lives, choosing to join the Military shortly after high school, they were dealt a shocking blow when Abigail collapsed at her work desk and was pronounced dead at the scene.

They later found out she had been fighting a private battle against lung cancer, having become a heavy smoker after the triplets' birth.

Surprisingly, even to himself, Gordon was the most openly affected by the tragedy. He had secretly hoped that he and Abigail could get back together someday when they were both in a better place. He had made an emergency trip back to Ohio, where he and his sons said goodbye to Abigail in a lonely, rainy cemetery, shortly before the triplets were shipped off to the Military.

Then, the visions started.

The Valley in his dreams looked real. He would watch as vivid, golden fire swept away mountains, and two beings of unmatched power clashed before whatever cosmic consciousness could be called God.

He woke up crying every time, wishing he could have seen more of the spectacle.

In the months before his confrontation with Benedict, the cowboy corpse would pay him regular visits. Always preceded by the scent of garlic, Gordon would see the silhouette out of the corner of his eye, just beyond reach. But it was in his bedroom, when he tried to return to the Valley, where the thing would wake him.

Its screaming maw would hover over him, its screech like something from another level of perception. The bloodshot eyes dangled limply from their sockets, perpetually looking down at him.

But reflex always drew him toward the phantom. He would feel an icy, electric tingle in his skin as he entered the darkness of its mind. Once inside, he was compelled to reflect on his worthless life, and was offered the chance to escape to the obsidian chasm that would serve as the conclusion of his being.

He would tell the thing its time was wasted on him.

Yet as the visions persisted, he needed answers, and he knew exactly where to get them.

DenCom had always been into odd research, and when the new CEO took over, he hadn't been very skilled at covering his tracks when it came to his investigations.

Benedict had obviously been investigating paranormal events, among other things, using the company's funds, so Gordon put in request after request for a meeting with Benedict to ask about his visions. He didn't care what his boss thought at this point. He didn't even care if he was fired for bringing up such an odd topic. He just wanted *something*.

After a particularly intense encounter with the phantom, he worked up the courage to burst into Benedict's office and demand answers.

The rest was obvious now to both of them. Von Gord was an insignificant man who had somehow tapped into one of the universe's best-kept secrets and had been punished for it. He had fought to be included among the elite few who knew of it, or at least knew enough to make sense of it.

Now, he would know everything.

"WHY DO YOU DO THIS?" HE WHISPERED TO BENEDICT.

The reason had never bothered Von Gord until now, until the end of his struggle to get answers. The simple question of why Benedict, Morecraft, and others like them investigated these things had never been his concern, but with Benedict refusing to answer anything else, he had to ask. "What do you have to gain?"

This made Benedict sit up straight.

His eyes grew dark and serious.

"You really wanna know?" he asked.

49

Monday, July 29th
Networking Hub 17
Denver, Colorado
4:48 PM (Mountain Time)

THE SCREEN ABOVE NELSON CLICKED ON, AND AS THE IMAGE APPEARED, THE BLURRED FORMS OF THE GROUP IN VON GORD'S HOUSE BECAME VISIBLE.

Nelson gave a quick, excited slap to the side of the desk, making both Aron and Andrea jump.

"We got in! I have the feed!" he exclaimed.

The pair sat up in their seats and watched the new display.

Nelson had broken through Von Gord's defenses without incident. He now had access to and control of the system. Everything Von Gord could see or do would be because Nelson allowed it. The connection was strong, and he used this to take advantage of one variable: A webcam.

The image was rough, the camera slowly focusing on the room, the image resolution rising and giving them greater clarity. They could see Michael's silhouette behind a couch, and who they thought was Benedict slouched across the cushions on his left side, staring into the eyes of a man in a wheelchair with two men to his right—Von Gord and his sons.

"We should have audio any second now," Nelson said as he focused on another screen. "The airstrike is ready to go. They have one minute to get out."

"One minute!" Aron repeated in shock.

"But how are they getting out?" Andrea asked.

"Once our people create a distraction," Nelson replied, "they'll know what to do."

As an oppressive tension filled Networking Hub 17, they all watched Benedict struggle to sit up on the couch as the webcam audio came through.

"*I search*—"

"–FOR THE TRUTH, USING MY INVESTIGATORS AND MYSELF AS SOMETHING OF A MESSAGE TO ANYONE WHO MIGHT SHOW UP AFTER WE'RE GONE. I'm keeping a record, a collection of all of mankind's obscure accomplishments. Not things like the fall of nations or the eradication of disease, or even the majority of scientific discoveries our species has made. This is a testament to the *legends*, the things that no one—not even me—believed in or wanted to find. It's proof to anyone in the future, after we've been dead for tens or hundreds of years, who asks about what we did. It's a resume for those who want to know us, and a big middle finger to those who didn't think we could have done it. Well, we did. We conquered belief, and we conquered legends."

Benedict took in a breath, then slumped back in his

seat.

Von Gord looked like he was trying to frown. "And it's still not the right time for the truth to be known?"

"Not until it's done," Benedict replied. "And if I have it my way, it won't be done until I'm gone."

Von Gord seemed far from convinced.

"Well, that's very noble of you," he said to Benedict. "And I will let you have your wish. You'll be dead before it's ever seen."

Von Gord signaled to Michael, who looked him right in the eye as he gave the order. "You've earned it, Michael."

He didn't understand what Von Gord was implying at first, then reality hit him as the brothers drew away, back toward the computer. His hand fell to his back pocket.

To his gun.

Von Gord's tone became softer, gentler, but still with a hint of aggression.

"You've brought him to us and made this great day possible. You deserve the honor of erasing this *scum* from existence. Our Russian friends will thank you. The General will give you protection, if you so wish. This is for you, Mr. Ridding, our gift to—"

The computer came to life, and Michael knew what he had to do.

David, Evans, and Von Gord all turned around in unison. Benedict sat up straight as a message was displayed across the screens:

ALL FILES UPLOADED. READY FOR ACCESS.

Before Von Gord could act, a frantic call came in from the radio.

"*Von Gord*!" screamed one of the guards. "*We have incoming, it looks like a—!*"

An explosion rocked the front of the house, a fireball bellowing up behind the curtains, illuminating the room in a piercing, blinding orange. Von Gord shielded his eyes from the light, and David took hold of his father's wheelchair, ready to run.

Evans hadn't finished reading the screen when his head exploded.

Michael watched in disgust as the first man he had ever killed slumped over the keyboard bank and fell with a thud to the ground, blood splattering on the monitors from the stump of his neck as he dropped.

Still in shock from having taken his first life, Michael was unable to claim David's. Before the massive man could pull his gun out and fire, Michael had put one bullet in his arm, then another in the center of his chest. David fell back against the wall, his face a huffing, red mess as Benedict took the chance to dart out of the room. Michael followed right behind.

VON GORD TRIED TO YELL, TRIED TO ORDER DAVID TO GO AFTER THEM, BUT SHOCK HAD MADE HIS OUTBURST COME OUT AS A DRY, SHOCKED GASP.

He couldn't think, couldn't breathe as he looked at the monitors to see the new image that had replaced the file screen, slightly obscured by his son's blood.

An animated, eight-bit skeleton cowboy in a brown vest and blue pants shifted up and down the screen as its mouth opened and closed. A deep, electronic laugh filled the room.

He stared at it, never noticing David stumbling for the staircase, or even the deep roar of the incoming airstrike.

Von Gord could only focus on the skeleton's outstretched hands, thrust at him with both middle fingers extended. A message was written below:

```
The Valley Burns
```

The second missile burst through the window behind him. It flew across the room and pierced Von Gord's lower back through the wheelchair, passing through his gut and tearing him apart in an eruption of flesh before exploding on impact with the monitor bank.

50

MICHAEL AND BENEDICT BURST OUT OF THE HOUSE JUST AS THE SECOND MISSILE EXPLODED, CAREFUL TO AVOID FLAMING DEBRIS AS THEY WENT. The doors and porch at the front of the house had been destroyed, a gaping, flaming hole in their place. They leaped over the burning wreckage, then bolted straight for the *Bluestream*.

Michael looked back as the second-story window exploded. He couldn't see the F16 that Benedict had told him to expect, but he heard the quick, unfamiliar roar as the aircraft rocketed back into the sky.

As they raced for the *Bluestream*, one of the pilots stared from the open cabin door in shock. Benedict reached the plane first and ordered them to take off as soon as possible, the pilot forgoing any questions he might have had once he sensed the urgency in his superior's voice.

As Michael reached the plane, he stole one last look back at the house.

His stomach dropped.

David was chasing after them, assault rifle in hand,

firing a flurry of shots at the plane.

Michael hurried in, avoiding the barrage of bullets as Benedict frantically gave the order to: "Turn it around! Turn it around! Turn this damn plane around and get the hell out of here!" The pilots gave no protest.

David was close now, shooting at near point-blank range as the *Bluestream* turned around to face the runway. As bullets ricocheted and left little more than dents in the *Bluestream*'s hull, David tried to work his way around to the back of the plane. Michael was afraid that he knew David's plan: To shoot out the engines.

Not concerned for their attacker's safety, the pilots didn't think twice before pushing the engines to their limit.

THE FORCE FROM THE ACCELERATION SENT DAVID TOPPLING OVER BACKWARD AS HIS GUN FIRED WILDLY INTO THE AIR. He came to a stop in time to see the *Bluestream* lift into the air and fly out of sight.

As darkness took him, the house caved into the power of the fire that consumed it. While it collapsed, a crash could be heard throughout the small valley caused by the immense weight coming down to Earth, like some ancient monster letting out one last cry before dying.

But this monster was far from dead.

51

Tuesday, July 30ᵗʰ
Seyðisfjörður, Iceland
7:32 PM (Iceland Time)

MICHAEL WAS ENJOYING HIS FIRST QUIET MOMENT SINCE THE ORDEAL AT VON GORD'S.

The *Bluestream* was in poor shape after leaving the mansion in flames twelve hours ago. They were able to land the plane safely at a small airport in Iceland, but they had no means to repair it.

Still, Benedict had his people, and he was confident the plane would fly again in good time, but that still left him and Michael stranded in Iceland.

They were directed to a small cruise liner that would take them from Seyðisfjörður in Iceland to Hirtshals in Denmark, where they would then catch a flight home. Although it was not Michael or Benedict's preferred means of travel, it did lend itself to three days of much-needed relaxation.

In Denmark, things would get much more complex.

From Hirtshals, they would need to take a train to Aalborg before catching a flight to Amsterdam. Then, after spending nearly three hours waiting in the airport, they would board a flight that would take them back to Denver.

Once stateside, they would part ways, Michael catching a flight back to Palm Springs, and Benedict returning home for what he proclaimed would be "a week of anime and chill unlike any experienced by mortal men."

It promised to be an interesting trip. Still, they knew that if they had the choice, they would have taken the private jet, instead.

Michael promised himself that, upon returning home, he would take time off from everything and rest for a while. He would finally give his body the chance to heal and begin what he knew would be weeks, if not months, of self-reflection.

He had killed a man, tried to kill another, and he didn't want to think about it ever again. The stress of the trip ahead and his present physical discomfort acted only as distractions from his guilt.

But he didn't know if it was right to feel guilty. He killed in self-defense. He had to believe that.

Right or wrong, it was done, and by some miracle of God, the plan had worked. He didn't want to admit he felt even the least bit of regret.

But in his first moment alone, he couldn't avoid it.

Michael stood at the railing of the cruise ship, his new coat blowing in the gentle breeze as he watched the retreating Icelandic shoreline. He had given in and bought a long, black wool coat similar to Benedict's. While he had anticipated his friend cracking jokes about how they were now "twinning," all Benedict had said was that it fit him nicely.

Oranges and purples danced along the ship's wake. As the day came to an end, he could see the sun's reflection reaching toward him in the water, like some golden path beckoning him, leading to that forsaken Valley.

As the ship moved further out to sea, Michael realized that this was his first moment alone in days. He had been in the care of doctors, psychopaths, friends, or his cat, but he'd never been given time to himself. The constant supervision had been hard for him, and he was glad it was almost over as he pulled the gun out from his coat pocket.

He had bought the thing years ago for home defense, but it was only now that he felt the gravity of the weapon, the weight and responsibility it carried, for the first time. He didn't blame it as some people might have. It had saved his life—his and Benedict's—but he didn't feel any attachment to it. The gun was an object, and only an object. So, as he gently tossed it over the stern of the ship, he felt no loss. It hit the water and sank like a stone, the tiny ripples lost in the boat's wake.

"Couldn't have gotten it home, anyway."

Michael hadn't noticed Benedict next to him until he had spoken; apparently, he was never truly alone.

Neither said a word as the sun sank below the horizon, taking the bright colors of the ocean with it. Neither knew what to say. Several minutes later, though, Michael finally broke the silence.

"I'm sorry."

"Huh?" Benedict looked at him.

"I'm sorry, Benedict," Michael admitted again, now looking down at the water. "Back at my place, all of this... I shouldn't have been so... *harsh*."

"Michael, you did exactly what you needed to and exactly what I wanted you to," Benedict reassured him. "You did good."

Michael was unconvinced. Sure, they'd gotten out alive. The act hadn't been easy, but it had worked in their favor in the face of death, which they had both narrowly avoided, thanks to Benedict. All things considered, though, the things that Michael had seen and done, everything he had been through in the past week, would haunt him for years, maybe for the rest of his life.

"Then, I need you to promise me something." Michael turned to Benedict. "I *never* want to be involved in... *operations* like this again. I thought Antarctica would be enough for me, but now that people's lives are at stake, I can't afford to be your patsy anymore. I'll keep working for you, don't get me wrong, but I won't be the 'yes man' you want me to be, not if this is where it leads."

Benedict looked away. "I can't promise that, Michael."

Michael didn't respond. He only waited until Benedict faced him again.

"All this stuff," Benedict began, "the Valley, your unrelated investigations, DenCom... they all carry the obvious risk that someone will want to stop us. That being said, I know of two major movements that would target you, the worst of which I am doing my best to prepare for. We got a brief glimpse of the lesser today, at least that's what it sounded like. According to my sources, it looks like the Russian group that supported Von Gord is getting ready for a large-scale terrorist attack on the United States, and DenCom is number one on their hitlist. This will most likely mean that you're in the direct line of fire. But if we lose this war, it won't make a difference whether or not you're working for DenCom. Your life as an American would change forever. At least, under DenCom, you have some control over the outcome. Until now, we believed that the Russian group was years away from posing a real threat, but now, we know different, and we'll act on it and stop them."

"But that won't be the end of it."

Benedict hesitated. "As far as you're concerned, after the Russian group is taken care of, the threats to you and your friends and family should be nonexistent. I know for a fact that the second group won't be mobilizing for a very long time, and I can handle them on my own. But these people, Von Gord's partners, are determined to bring down DenCom and discredit the United States in any way possible. Von Gord is far from the worst we'll see of them because unlike him, the Russians aren't concerned with the Valley. They only agreed to work with him because he had the power to bring DenCom—and me—down. His reasons were not their concern. From now on, until this group is bombed into oblivion, we'll be playing by their rules. In other words, we'll be fighting a war. They're not going to care about conspiracy theories or what kind of cryptids we're hiding or what have you. All they want is me, you, and everyone else at DenCom out of the way. And I know you're not going to like this, but people like us— people like you—are the only ones on the front lines who can stop them."

"But why me? Why DenCom?"

"Because... because we are the only thing standing between them and a full-scale invasion of the United States."

Michael's jaw dropped. "What about the government? The FBI, CIA, Military?"

"They rely on us for tech and support, along with intelligence, in some cases. We're the supplier of the majority of the government's technological forces, some of its most advanced mobile weaponry. Didn't you ever wonder how DenCom could have such a large sphere of influence and be as financially successful as it is without going commercial? We're the framework for most of the major divisions of the government, the very foundation they stand on, as well as the basement where they hide all their secrets. Someday, I'll show you exactly how much we make and do, but for now, I'm bound to secrecy. All I can say is that if they take us down, it'll leave the door wide open for an all-out invasion from land, sea, air, and digital fronts."

"So, we're technically government agents?" Michael asked, thinking back to the times they had been given unhindered access to locations normally inaccessible to the public and conducted investigations unquestioned by the authorities. He remembered how easily Benedict received help and "favors" from the President and how he had used the FBI badge to get them down Mt. San Jacinto. It was all beginning to make sense. "We're not just your personal investigators?"

"You're whatever you need to be," Benedict said. "If you need to be an FBI agent, I'll make a call. If you need to be a paranormal researcher who wants five million dollars to dredge Loch Ness, you'll have it."

"Because we were selected," Michael recalled.

Benedict sighed. "More like drafted," he replied. "Just like me."

They didn't speak for a while after, instead watching the stars slowly appear in the night sky.

In the silence, they both knew where they stood. They were soldiers for some unknown but persuasive force. And neither could leave it, couldn't leave *Him*. Death was the only other option.

And death was the last thing Benedict needed to discuss with Michael.

More than ready for the longest day of his life to be over, Michael turned and headed back to the double doors that led to the staterooms.

However, Benedict spoke again, just before he left earshot.

"I talked with Nelson before I came out here," he started. "As you know, he's one of my most trusted allies. He keeps track of things very dear to me, one of those being my last will and testament."

Michael turned around slowly.

"Years ago, I had him add a protective clause," Benedict continued, "something to keep you and the company safe in case I happen to... well, for lack of a better term, go totally insane. Given what I'm studying, I fear it's a reasonable risk. So... I need someone I can trust to... kill me, if or when such a thing should happen. I can be weird and kooky all I want, but..." He hesitated. "If I ever get ... crazy—like the bad kind of crazy, the kind that makes me do what I did to Von Gord, except... worse..." He took a few deep breaths, occasionally licking his lips. "I need to be stopped. My will states that I would accept my fate, even if, at the time, I wouldn't be in the right frame of mind to do so, and also that no one would be punished for doing what was necessary. For the longest time, Nelson was the only one on that list, but today, I added you."

Benedict approached him. "I know you don't want to kill again, but I *need* you on that list. Unlike Nelson, you've seen the results of my, well, handiwork, and it pains me to admit that I've done worse to people I loved because no one could stop me. But I trust you to put me down, if and when the time comes."

Michael didn't respond as Benedict walked past him and through the double doors. As they shut behind him, Michael didn't know what to think. The task he had been given weighed heavy on him, but in it, he saw something else:

Benedict *trusted* him.

He didn't want to think about it, not if he wanted to get any sleep. For his own good, Michael decided to let it go.

The job was there, and if he had to, he would do it.

Clearing his mind, he let his only concerns be what to have for dinner and if the television in his room got the Weather Channel.

52

ARON AND ANDREA MADE IT TO THE HOTEL IN THE STILL DARK EARLY MORNING. They had stayed with Nelson through the Greenland night until Michael and Benedict had worked out their travel arrangements. When everything was settled, Nelson encouraged them to get some sleep at the hotel. Michael and Benedict were safe; all they had left to do now was get home. He promised to keep them updated if anything changed, so they agreed to get some rest.

They lumbered into the hotel room and fell onto their respective beds, begging sleep to take them. However, it claimed neither of them, no matter how much they wished it.

As dawn came, Andrea was the first to give up.

She forced herself off the bed and told Aron she was going to take a quick shower. Aron took the opportunity to change into his sleeping pants and a white tank top, then lay back on the bed to try and calm his mind.

Suddenly, Aron's cell phone rang. Aron was afraid that it meant bad news, but what bad news could there possibly be? Evans had been killed, Von Gord burned with the house, and David was reportedly dead on the tarmac. What else was there to be afraid of?

Thankfully, his fears were misplaced.

"Aron, just thought you should know that it's going to take them a few days to get back. I can't get them a flight on this short of notice, so they're going to have to take a boat to Denmark and go from there."

Aron sighed. It was a setback but, thankfully, not a huge one. He knew Michael and Benedict would be okay— they had the resources they needed to get home—but Aron couldn't shake the feeling that something was still dreadfully wrong.

"All right, I'll talk with Andrea and see if she wants to stay a few more days." He couldn't resist prodding further. "Is there anything else going on we should be concerned about?"

"Well..." Nelson trailed off, thinking over the right way to explain yet another dilemma to Aron, who was already worried all over again. "The security system in Benedict's house is causing us some concern. He said Von Gord had a tap, which I'm working on removing now, but there's something else. We've gotten alerts of a break-in. I sent our people over to investigate, but they haven't found anything, so, for now, we're thinking it's a glitch in the system."

"Nothing visual?"

"Not that I've seen. The motion sensors were going off in the living room, hallway, and bedroom, one right after the other, like someone was walking through the house. But no doors were opened, and nothing was caught on camera, so I think it's just a bug," Nelson explained, which was almost enough to settle Aron's nerves.

"All right. I think I'll be up for a while, so give us a call if anything changes," Aron said.

"Will do. I'll see you in time," Nelson said, and they hung up.

53

ANDREA SAT ON THE SHOWER FLOOR, CURLED INTO A BALL AS WATER GENTLY FELL OVER HER.

She had heard the phone ring, but since Aron wasn't banging on the door, she knew it couldn't be important.

Time flew as she fruitlessly tried to let the water rinse her anxiety away. The past few days had been stressful—much more stressful than usual—but, as always, she had tried to focus more on doing what she could to help, bottling up her emotions until she could no longer handle the pressure.

She knew it was childish, but it described exactly what had happened over the past few days: The terrorist attacks that had almost killed her friends, being flown out to Denver with Aron for their own safety and to help Nelson, watching Benedict and Michael almost die in Greenland... it'd been too much for her to handle, but she couldn't afford to show it. For Benedict's sake, for Michael's sake, for Aron's sake... the last thing she needed to be right now was a sobbing mess.

But here, in the shower of some random hotel room in Denver, Colorado, that was all she could afford to be. It was childish, sure, but she forced herself to excuse it. Not only because she knew she and her friends could be childish at times, but in her situation, anyone would be.

There was a knock on the door a little while later,

snapping Andrea back to reality. What did Aron want? Maybe Nelson had called to tell them that something else had gone wrong...

"Yeah?"

Her quick reply was met with a calm yet concerned voice.

"You doing okay?" Aron asked through the door. "You've been in there nearly an hour."

"Yeah," Andrea replied, quickly pulling herself together. "Just lost track of time."

"All right. Just wanted to make sure you didn't fall asleep or something."

"I couldn't *possibly* be that lucky," she replied, and she could faintly hear Aron laugh as he walked away.

Andrea shakily stood up, immediately regretting doing so as her legs protested the sudden motion and weight.

She didn't want to come out yet. She didn't want to face him until she was ready.

But she also didn't want to deal with her fear alone.

Don't even think about it, she told herself. *You could ruin everything*.

She couldn't let the thought go. It had been years since she had someone close, having abstained from romantic relationships after her last one had ended so painfully. Last time, it had been no one's fault; there had been no goodbye. There had only been a silhouette against the late-night lights of L.A., suspended above the city like a god.

She didn't want to let him in, to turn the simple desire for support and comfort into something more.

She opened the door, dressed in an old band shirt and a pair of sweat shorts. Aron lay in his bed, his eyes closed, but she could tell he was still awake. She looked at him, seeing plenty she liked but nothing new.

She still saw someone she called a friend, someone she could share her pain with, someone she could talk to and learn from.

Someone who, deep inside, needed the same thing she did.

Cringing, she caved.

"Aron?" she asked softly.

His head rose, his eyes gazing past her.

"Could you... move over a bit?"

Aron hesitated. He clearly wasn't sure if he heard correctly.

Then, he took one look at her red-rimmed eyes and understood. He moved over and gave Andrea room to lie down.

She lay with her back to him, her damp brown hair spreading across the pillow. She felt his residual body heat around her, and her fear slowly melted away, replaced by the comforting knowledge that she wasn't alone.

"Can you...?" Andrea hesitated, wondering if her next question would take things too far.

But, as if he had read her mind, Aron moved closer. He reached over, letting his right hand come to rest on her left shoulder. Then he slid his still-aching left arm under her and wrapped her in a tight hug.

Before Aron could worry that he had misunderstood, Andrea let her own arms wrap around his, and her body relaxed.

Their worries drifted off into space. As she grew drowsy, Andrea spoke only once more before sleep finally came. The statement was true, yet laced with her familiar, friendly sarcasm.

"If you tell Michael or Benedict, I'll kick your ass."

Aron couldn't help but laugh.

"I won't."

And then, finally, they slept.

54

"*YA AIN'T DONE YET*," SPOKE THE SOFT TEXAN VOICE. "*Not while I still linger.*"

David's eyes searched the blurry world around him, his head unable to move. He was immobile, the deepest sleep he'd known leaving him paralyzed, but he barely recognized his surroundings as home.

What he didn't recognize was the pair of black cowboy boots inches from his face.

"*I'm in need of some assistance, Mr. Gordon.*"

David couldn't look any further up, but he felt it odd that the man was calling him by his last name. No one had called him that in years, not since his father had taken on the name Von Gord. But this man spoke the word with a grain of respect that was overshadowed by intimidation.

"*M' faith in him grows weak... frail.*"

Him? Who was "him"? Who was this man?

"*Your father may'a had the right idea. Benedict's bin keepin' things to himself, even from me.*"

David's eyes widened, not at the man's words, but at the blurry yellow serpent slithering into his field of view, gliding along with a self-aware grace that no animal should possess. The snake's head rose onto the black boot, and it proceeded to slither up the man's leg, its rattling tail sounding off infrequently as the man spoke.

"I'm growin' tired of his games. Help me remind him who holds the straight flush, and I'll personally welcome you t' the Valley m'self."

Consciousness began to return. Life poured in unnaturally. Inhumanly.

"Get on up, now."

As David's vision cleared, the man vanished into thin air.

DAVID WOKE UP IN THE GROWING LIGHT OF THE FOLLOWING MORNING. The fires had long since died, his father's home now a smoking pile of charred wood and ash.

But David wasn't in much better shape.

He tried to get to his feet, but pain forced him to his knees.

Pure, raw, unobstructed *pain*.

The bullet wounds in his arm and chest stung from where Ridding had shot him. His broken leg was now unprotected, the splint having shattered when he was blown down the runway. And, to top it all off, there was a burning pain in his back and stomach unlike any he had ever felt in his life. For all he knew, it was probably from when Sanderson had rammed him with the Pantera at the Spectrum six days ago.

Or had it been seven?

He didn't know how long he'd been unconscious, but he knew it was morning. A cool, humid breeze and the sounds of birds chirping sat in sharp contrast to the hellish scene around him. He had spent an entire night, at the very least, lying unconscious on the tarmac. He needed to get moving.

David's first thought was to search the remains of the house and find his father and brother so he could bury them. But how could he manage to dig two graves, especially in his current condition? Still, he had a feeling that it was already too late. He could hear the rubble moving and shifting, as if something was trying to dig its way in—or *out*. David tried to push the thought away, blaming the noises on the rubble settling instead of the rats coming to eat what little flesh was left on his family's bones.

The mental image of the latter made him want to vomit.

After all they had done, after everything their family had sacrificed to get to this point, a lunatic and a fish store owner had managed to beat them.

Managed to beat *him*.

David felt personally responsible for his family's death. They had trusted him as the leader of the operation, and he had proven to be an inexperienced, unseasoned fool.

He needed to make it up to them.

Only one idea came to him. A fantastic, stupid idea. But was it possible? His father's computer was gone, but had it taken their last weapon, their last resort with it? Or was it backed up by the systems in the outbuilding?

It had been years since he'd called on his coding and hacking skills, and he hadn't actively practiced them since high school. While his father had made him practice on occasion, David feared he didn't have the necessary skills to execute the plan, but that little voice with a Texan twang far in the back of his mind told him it could be done, that, if necessary, it would point him in the right direction and make sure that, for once, everything worked perfectly.

But would he be able to control the temperamental program?

It was unstable, especially if they still wanted to take Benedict alive.

But David didn't care about that.

He didn't care what the Russians thought.

He only cared about avenging his father and brothers.

Without his father, he was alone. Those Russian bastards wouldn't give him anything else since he had failed. They would be along soon to gather up any and all evidence of their involvement with the Gordon family, and David knew they would consider him a loose end. It was foolish to think that they would keep him alive after everything he had failed to do.

And after what he was about to do.

Possibly one of their greatest weapons, unleashed before its time. They would never have the chance to use it again, and David was just fine with that. He didn't figure he'd be around to see his punishment, anyway.

One final push. One last try to end the madness.

One last stand.

Using his assault rifle as a crutch, David limped to the outbuilding that, since it had posed no obvious threat, had been left untouched by the airstrike.

But it took hours, his unrelenting agony turning what should have been a short walk into an odyssey fueled only by his determination and burning hatred.

Finally, his hunched-over form reached the outbuilding. It was a storage building, mostly holding weaponry and spare parts for their allies' efforts in Siberia.

But there was something else inside: The backup computer.

It was David's last hope.

55

MICHAEL AND BENEDICT ARRIVED IN AMSTERDAM LATE THAT NIGHT, LEAVING A TWO-HOUR WINDOW BEFORE THEY COULD BOARD THEIR FLIGHT HOME. Their passports and paperwork, adjusted to reflect the last several days' travel, had been waiting for them in Hirtshals, courtesy of President Robinson.

Once inside the airport, Benedict spent the majority of the time either on the phone with Nelson or looking through one of the small bookstores. Michael, who was listening to reefing podcasts while they waited, only caught snippets of Benedict's conversations.

From what he could gather, the security alerts in Benedict's home hadn't stopped, even after Nelson had removed Von Gord's tap. They were working together to try and resolve the issue, but nothing seemed to come of it. The bug in the motion sensors had been contained to the bedroom, but it was trying to track someone standing at the foot of Benedict's bed and occasionally glitched into the doorway. After three attempts to find someone,

Benedict's onsite security team was ready to give up and tell Benedict to invest in a new system. The call ended with Benedict heading off to the nearby bookstore, probably to clear his head.

Benedict returned with a small shopping bag just as their flight began pre-boarding calls. They made their way onto the massive A380 and settled into the second-level first class compartment for the long overnight flight. Michael took the window seat; Benedict, the aisle.

Michael lay back in his seat, covering himself with a complimentary blanket. Benedict removed a paperback, as well as a book lamp and pair of reading glasses, from the shopping bag. The sight almost made Michael want to crack a joke before they took off.

They both had a small steak dinner before Michael fell asleep and Benedict returned to his book, but not before ordering a small glass of whiskey. Benedict wasn't a drinking man; he never had been. He had no strong feelings or love for alcohol, but after the absolute hell he had been through, he felt he deserved to cut loose a little.

But, as always, one drink would be it. He was never exactly sober to begin with. He didn't want to know what kind of drunk he would be.

Now settled with a book in one hand and drink in the other, Benedict relaxed for what he hoped would be a long, uneventful flight.

56

ARON AND ANDREA CHOSE TO STAY IN DENVER UNTIL MICHAEL AND BENEDICT WERE BACK IN THE STATES. Andrea had managed Modern Aquaria from her phone, and Granger was being cared for by a zoo assistant. Michael's fish needed little attention since the feeders were automatic, and the water quality was being monitored by a sensor in each tank.

Everything considered, all was well in Palm Springs: The fish shop was doing well, the search for the terrorists had "supposedly" ended in the discovery of a double suicide deep in the woods, and they even heard that repairs to the tram were beginning soon. Only the valley station had suffered major damage, and it was already in the early stages of reconstruction. Spokesmen had said that they hoped to be open again, this time with a heavy increase in security, in time for the winter season.

Even the *Bluestream* was on its way to recovery. Benedict had flown his own people to Iceland to fix the plane, and they said it would be flyable before the end of the month.

To celebrate, Aron and Andrea were enjoying a late-night room service dinner of shrimp and steak. Their time together had been the break they didn't know they needed, and they were sad to see it end. But it would end the following day, when they would catch an evening flight back to Orange County. They would drive back to Palm Springs in Andrea's car and return to their daily lives by the next morning.

Everything seemed to be turning around.

Then, Nelson called.

Aron picked up the phone, expecting Nelson to inform them of a delay or minor hiccup in the plan.

"David's gone," was all he said.

Aron choked on his wine and nearly dropped the glass. But he managed to control himself and ask Nelson what he meant.

"I was planning the recon flight to examine the state of Von Gord's compound, but when I got the most recent satellite images in, David's body was gone. There's no trace. Nothing! It's like he just got up and walked away!"

Aron felt numb.

"But he had to be dead," Aron replied.

Andrea was catching on; she shot up to get herself ready for the inevitable drive to DenCom Tower.

"Aron, he *was* dead—that's what all the readings said! And even if it was a glitch, he should've bled out in the night. This shouldn't be possible!"

"Maybe someone came and got him?"

"I didn't see any sign of it, but I'll keep looking."

"All right, we'll be there as soon as Loose can pick us up."

Nelson told him when and where to be, and they hung up.

57

Friday, August 1st
40,000 Feet above the Atlantic Ocean
12:52 AM (Eastern Time)

THEY HAD BEEN FLYING FOR JUST OVER FOUR HOURS WHEN BENEDICT NOTICED THAT THE STEWARDESSES WERE MUCH MORE ACTIVE THAN USUAL. As he casually glanced up from his book, he could see them sporting worried looks, concerned about something. While they huddled near the cockpit door, Benedict tried to brush it off as something insignificant. The thought of anything more serious than a shortage of peanuts—which was a real concern that Benedict actually had—never crossed his mind.

Soon after he first noticed the odd behavior, a phone in the kitchen rang once before a stewardess immediately picked it up. Benedict couldn't hear the conversation, but he could tell by the woman's face that she wasn't receiving good news.

Then, he saw her look directly at him.

As Benedict looked back to the novel, she sat the phone on the counter. Then, she headed down the aisle toward him. He could now see how worried she really was; everyone except Benedict had fallen asleep hours ago, so she made no attempt to hide it. She quickly approached, careful not to wake the other passengers, then knelt beside his seat.

"Would you happen to be Benedict?" she whispered.

"Yes." He closed the novel and placed it in the seat pocket.

"I'm sorry to interrupt you, but I need you to come up front. There's an emergency call waiting for you."

Benedict wasted no time undoing his seat belt.

He tried to remain calm, but when faced with the worried flight attendants around him, his confusion and worry began to show. They escorted him to the kitchen area, where they shut the curtain behind him, separating them from the rest of the cabin. One of the stewardesses picked up the corded phone with a trembling hand and gave it to Benedict. He took it, nervous of what—or who—he would find on the other end.

He was not disappointed when he heard David's groggy voice.

"Hello, Benedict." His voice was strained, yet wispy. "I trust you're having a pleasant flight."

Benedict didn't react. He couldn't. What could he say? *Yeah, man, I feel great. Sorry about bombing your house and stuff, but I was having a really off day. We cool, bro?*

"Anyway, I'm glad we're talking," David continued, temporarily consumed by a wet coughing fit before he moved on. "You see, I gave you and Michael too much freedom, and you used it to kill my father and brothers. All because I didn't have the guts to keep you under control. Nor did I have the brains to see that Michael was going to turn on us, that he was with you all along. I should have seen it. I should have killed him once we had you. But I can't change that now. All I can do is avenge my family.

"Now, it's your turn to watch helplessly as everyone around you suffers."

Benedict remained silent.

"Do the stewardesses around you look nervous? Well, they should. Because the pilots are dead. And within the next two hours, this plane will crash into the Atlantic Ocean, taking you and Michael with it."

"What the hell are you—?"

"Our friends in Russia didn't want you to know what my father was creating—it could be the next step in warfare, beyond even DenCom's capabilities. He tried to create a virus that could take control of the *Bluestream*, or any other aircraft his allies saw fit. But it was traceable and could have led right to him, which is why it was designated as a last resort. And, to be frank, it was far too easy to track down your flight plans and upload this 'last resort' onto the plane's computer.

"The first step was to get rid of the pilots. Now, you would think an airtight cockpit would be a great idea if the rest of the plane lost pressure, right? Well, reverse it, and you have a wonderfully easy way to dispose of those flying the plane. For the virus, the next part was simple: Tell the plane to keep descending until it reached the Atlantic. After that... Well, if I had to guess, you wouldn't have much of a chance to get out of the plane before it sank. That is, if you managed to survive the impact. And don't count on any radios working or life rafts deploying —that would be *far* too easy."

His breathing heavy, Benedict fell back against the wall, then slowly slid down until he came to rest on the floor.

"My best advice would be to not try anything. If you do attempt to take control, the plane will only descend faster. The more you fight my father's creation, the shorter your trip will be. I suggest you spend your last hours thinking about what you've done."

Benedict was stunned. It all seemed so impossible. He only had one question left.

"Why are you doing this?"

"Because you just killed your last chance to get out of this alive. What little hope you had left burned with my father. And besides, if you really want to take your secrets to the grave, who am I to argue?"

"But everyone else on the plane—"

"Will welcome the Valley, as I am about to." A subtle click could be heard on the other end. "But I don't think I'll be seeing you there, will I?"

Before Benedict could respond, the line was filled with the loud report of a firearm. A thump soon followed.

As the stewardesses waited for a response, Benedict forced himself to his feet and placed the phone back on the receiver. Then, rushing past them, he hurried to Michael, who had managed to sleep through the whole thing.

As he knelt beside his friend, Benedict could already

feel the plane steadily descending.

58

Thursday, July 31st
Networking Hub 17
Denver, Colorado
11:42 PM (Mountain Time)

ARON AND ANDREA BURST THROUGH THE FRONT DOORS OF DENCOM TOWER, RACING PAST THE MAIN RECEPTION DESK.

They caught an empty elevator and were at their floor within a minute. The door to Networking Hub 17 was already wide open. They hurried to the desk where they found a worried, frantic Nelson at the controls. He was almost unrecognizable, compared to the mostly placid person they had met days ago.

"Contact has been lost with Michael and Benedict's flight," Nelson announced. "I just got word that the pilots aren't responding, and that radar has the plane heading off course and descending fast. It's traveling southwest over the Northern Atlantic, steadily turning south. It'll crash within two hours if something isn't done fast."

Nelson rushed back to the monitors with Aron and Andrea close behind. He sat and watched one line of code after another fly by on most of the screens. "I'm in contact with the FAA and the President's people. They want Michael and Benedict to assess the situation and report back, but I can't get them to answer my calls."

"What can we do from here?" Andrea asked.

In truth, Nelson didn't know the answer. He was stunned that something like this could happen. It wasn't part of the plan—*none* of this had been—but it had been so carefully laid out, protection so carefully established.

But Von Gord, along with his sons, had been the inconceivable variable. There was no way this should have been allowed to go as far as it had, except if...

Nelson's heart sank.

He fought not to convey the revelation only he understood, but suddenly it all made sense to him. For the first time, *it all made sense!*

He looked back to Andrea, filled with newfound energy.

"I can only relay the President's orders to them. He wants them to assess the situation and, if all else fails, try and get into the cockpit. From what the FAA has told me, there are no air marshals on the plane, so Benedict's FBI badge will have to do the trick. Maybe then, they can help the pilots land the plane somewhere on the coast."

59

MICHAEL WAS AWAKE AND FILLED IN ON THE SITUATION.

The first order of business was to get into the cockpit, which had an electronic lock that was sealed shut from the inside.

The crew didn't quite trust Michael or Benedict, knowing that they had some ties to the terrorists who had done this, but Benedict's FBI badge seemed to put them at ease. Pushing their suspicions aside, they knew they needed to work together to break into the cockpit. Without any weapons or air marshals on board, they had resorted to using the emergency fire axe. It would not be simple or quiet, but it was their only option.

With the first loud smack on the door hinges, the whole cabin was awake and aware that something was going on. Two of the stewardesses stood outside the closed curtains to address the issue, explaining that the cockpit door had jammed and that they needed to break through. It wasn't the whole truth, but it kept the cabin calm for the moment.

In the darkness outside, no one could see how low

they really were. Although still at a safe altitude, it was going to be obvious when the sun came up that they were in dire straits.

But Benedict doubted they would last that long.

After the first hinge was broken off, the second down below went much easier. His tired hands slipping, Michael almost gave up before the door fell off the hinges.

Air rushed into the cabin.

"Oh *fu*—!" Benedict was cut off by a series of coughs brought on by the repulsive scent that bombarded them.

The pilots were obviously dead, splayed about in their seats with respirators on, desperate for air in their final moments. A vomitous smell filled the cockpit, its origins left to their imaginations. The scene made them nauseous, but they couldn't leave yet.

With Benedict's help, Michael moved the crew's bodies from their seats and laid them behind the first officer's chair, out of sight from anyone who might try to get a closer look from the kitchen.

"Do you think we can make it to the mainland?" one of the stewardesses asked once the pilots were taken care of.

"If the virus is removed, someone can talk us through landing," Benedict replied, obviously favoring the most optimistic ending over the realistic one. "Michael, I'll see if I can get a hold of Nelson. He should be able to remove it, or at least help us down." He looked over his shoulder at the women behind him. "Is that 'no cell phone' rule still in effect?"

His attempt to lighten the mood was met with shaking heads and serious faces.

"All right, I'll give it a shot. Michael, get in the pilot's seat and one of you get in the first officer's. The rest of you keep watch over the cabin and try to keep everyone calm."

Benedict left Michael with the flight attendant, meeting the two others by the curtain outside. They'd just gotten settled in the cockpit as Benedict retrieved his cell phone and turned it on, ignoring the other passengers around him mumbling about a strange smell. It took a moment for the phone to boot up, and as it did, he walked back to the small kitchen outside the cockpit, taking a seat by the emergency door.

He was relieved to see he had ten missed calls, all from Nelson. So, they knew *something* was wrong, at least.

As he reached for the call back button, yet another call came in from Nelson.

"What's the situation?" Nelson asked, not waiting for Benedict to say a word. He filled Nelson in on all the gray areas—including the call from David and the fact that the pilots were dead—most of which he whispered as not to upset any eavesdropping passengers.

Nelson took several heavy breaths before he spoke. "All right, I've been in contact with the FAA. Two jets were scrambled a half hour or so ago. They should be able to guide you into Myrtle Beach. Over the last half hour, the plane has changed directions and is now heading southwest, sending you toward Florida or the Bahamas. It will take some work, but between myself and the FAA, we should be able to guide you down."

Benedict understood the plan, but he didn't feel the FAA was going to do much good in guiding the plane down. If he had to guess, they would be redirected to some suit who didn't understand the situation. Nelson had seen Von Gord's work firsthand and knew how long it could take to get through the weakest of his security. But this was a new animal, and they were already losing.

"Nelson," Benedict's voice was hushed further, so even the stewardesses couldn't hear him. "How could this happen?"

Nelson's matter-of-fact reply was also hushed. "I believe the agreement's been compromised, Sir."

Benedict didn't want to believe what he had just heard. But if it were true, there was next to no chance they were getting out of this alive.

Still, they had to try.

They needed someone on-site with Nelson who was as informed as possible and able to work with him until—

"Is Aron there?" Benedict asked.

There was rustling on the other end, soon followed by Aron's voice from a second headset.

"I'm here."

"Listen, can you guide us down?" Benedict asked.

"I... You know I only flew a Cessna, right?" Aron replied. "Something like this is *way* out of my league!"

"How far out?"

"I don't know... I only know the basics. It would be like telling a toddler to drive a tank!"

"But it could be done?" Nelson asked.

"Maybe, but it goes without saying that it's a horrible idea!"

"I need you to try," Benedict told him. "You're the only one who Nelson can directly filter commands through. In other words, you're the only one I trust to help us."

Everyone held their breath, waiting for Aron's response. It came as a small, quiet confirmation.

"All right."

"Good," Benedict said. "Nelson, how's the virus look?"

"Still fighting it off," Nelson replied. "I'm going to try to turn the plane west, back toward the States. After that, I'll try to override the descent command and we should have complete control."

"Good." Benedict looked at his clock. It had been almost forty minutes since David's call. "How high are we?"

"I've got you at just about 25,000 feet. You're moving parallel to the coast, just about 200 miles off."

"Lovely. Do you need to talk with Michael?"

"Not yet. He can't do anything until I override the virus. I've got a few things I'm going to try, so give me—"

The plane lurched forward, then plummeted into a nosedive.

The engines' roar came first. Then, Benedict could see and hear the first-class passengers begin to panic, screaming for their lives as debris and trash flew past them. Face masks deployed but were forced back to the ceiling as gravity took over. He heard Michael and the stewardess fighting against the g-forces, doing anything they could think of to stop the descent.

He could hear Nelson swearing at the computer, screaming at the program that fought him. He could tell that the man was using every bit of his superior intelligence to overcome the digital obstacles presented, as he was designed to do.

Slowly, the plane began to level off. Once the dive ended, everyone began reaching for masks except Benedict, who unbuckled and hurried to the cockpit.

"What the hell was that?" Benedict asked Nelson, trying to catch the breath he had lost.

"The virus. When I tried to go deeper, it fought back. But it looks like I broke the hold on the southern flight path. Now, I just have to break the descent... Oh, crap."

At Nelson's last statement, the cockpit came alive with flashing lights and alarms. Before Benedict could ask what it meant, Nelson updated him.

"The dive strained the engines. They're in bad shape —all four are smoking."

"*All* of them?!" Benedict repeated.

"All of them," Nelson confirmed.

"Well, that's just perfect," Benedict said to himself. Everyone in the cockpit looked at him. Benedict filled them in before returning to his call. "How far did we fall?"

"You lost about 5,000 feet. I've got you on course for Myrtle Beach, but at this rate, you'll hit the water about fifty miles off the coast."

Benedict repeated this information to everyone else,

and no one took the news well. Several of the flight attendants were clearly on the verge of a meltdown.

Admittedly, Benedict wasn't far behind.

He thought he was done with all this. He thought that the whole thing would go silent for a while after Von Gord's death. But no, David just *had* to have the last word. He just *had* to use his father's backup plan to take him down. And then, he had the nerve to off himself before Benedict could personally take part in more "interrogations."

He would never do what he did to Von Gord again—nothing like it. But so help him God, if he ever got ahold of the maniac who ran the show in Russia, he would shove his foot so far up their ass that whoever could pull it out would be crowned King of the Britons.

Dizziness hit him. He returned to his seat and looked out the window again, now seeing a dark form in the moonlight. He could make out the silhouette of a fighter jet rimmed in white light just off the wing. Although he couldn't see the opposite wing, he was sure the jet's twin was present.

"I can see the escorts," Benedict said. "Now what?"

Nelson and Aron had a short, muffled conversation on the other end of the line. When they came back on, Nelson was speaking.

"The flight's only about half full, right?"

"Yeah, I think so," Benedict said. The late-night trip probably hadn't been desirable to the majority of lower-end passengers, which Benedict now fully understood.

"Get everyone to the front of the plane, just as a precaution," Nelson replied. "If we need to do a water landing, Michael will need to put the plane down tail-first. Once everyone's up front, I'll try to further disengage the descent command. After that... Well, we'll know where you guys are."

"All right. I'll call back when we have everyone ready," Benedict said.

The two hung up for what Benedict feared could be the last time.

He got up from his seat and updated everyone on the plan. Then, he and the remaining flight attendants began herding the passengers to the front of the plane. As Benedict helped them start from the back, he couldn't help but notice the fear in everyone's eyes. None of them knew that he would be the one responsible for their deaths, simply by being among them.

He looked out the window to see how close the ocean was in the night sky, getting brief glimpses beneath the cloud cover and black smoke pouring from the engines.

60

THE LAST HALF HOUR HAD BEEN SPENT GATHERING AND MOVING THE PASSENGERS TO THE FRONT SEATS OF THE PLANE.

Although it was only half full, it still took time for the two hundred or so people to clear out of the back and settle themselves into front seats.

Once the passengers were seated, Benedict returned to the cockpit to update everyone on the development. Before calling Nelson, he made the grave mistake of taking another look out the window.

They were much lower now. Benedict got a quick glimpse of the still small waves, knowing he shouldn't be seeing as much detail as he was. As they began to skim the cloud cover, Benedict dialed Nelson.

"Everyone up front?" Nelson asked. After Benedict confirmed this, Nelson continued, "Good. Now, hand the phone to Michael. Have him hold it in place with the headset."

Benedict didn't understand at first, but then he saw the pair of headphones that Michael had placed around his neck in case they reestablished radio contact. Benedict positioned the phone between Michael's right ear and the headphone, which held it firmly in place.

"GET BUCKLED IN," MICHAEL SAID TO BENEDICT, LOOKING AT HIS FRIEND FOR WHAT HE HOPED WOULDN'T BE THE LAST TIME.

Benedict looked back with a mix of sadness and hope on his face. Then, he gave a simple salute and returned to his chair, strapping himself in tightly.

Michael took in a deep breath, then let it come out slowly and calmly.

Ready or not, it was time to end this.

"I'm going to hand you over to Aron," Nelson said. "He's going to help you down while I fight off the virus. The jets will follow and act as guides if you need them, so just say the word."

"Got it," Michael confirmed.

Static filled the other end as Aron returned to the conversation.

"You ready, Michael?" he said, sounding as worried as anyone on the plane.

"As I'll ever be," Michael replied.

For a moment that seemed to last forever, the plane was silent, barring the distorted, irregular rumble of the engines.

"All right," Aron said.

"I'm heading in no—"

Michael never heard the end of Nelson's statement.

Every light in the cockpit came alive. Alarms screamed in unison as the plane began to roll to the right, soon followed by the nose slowly, almost gently dipping downward.

Outside, the pilots of the fighter jets could only watch in horror as the plane performed a slow barrel roll. Followed by another... and another... again and again as the aircraft descended.

Smoke flew from the screaming engines, soon followed by a flurry of sparks and fire. As the plane's roll accelerated and the nosedive became steeper, the jets were forced to pull away from the falling aircraft. The pilots looked back only once to see the plane trailing a flurry of sparks and spinning columns of black smoke, marking its path as it disappeared beneath the clouds.

61

"I CAN'T CONTROL IT!" MICHAEL YELLED THROUGH THE PHONE.

The virus was fighting him. Fighting them all.

In Networking Hub 17, Aron frantically talked Michael through options to stop the roll.

Nelson almost had control, but the virus held on like a predator desperately trying to anchor its teeth into its helpless victim's neck. He was able to see that the plane was becoming unstable: Alarms were blaring through the speakers on the monitors. If the plane took much more of this, it would break apart, shatter like glass.

Aron poured information to Michael.

Michael reported back failure after failure.

Andrea could do no more than watch and pray.

Finally, with one massive push from Nelson, the virus sputtered, coughed, and died before him.

But by then, it was too late.

THEY BROKE THROUGH THE CLOUDS, THEIR LEFT WING DIPPING TO ONE SIDE AS MICHAEL FINALLY TOOK CONTROL OF THE PLANE. It was leveling out, but far too low.

They were only 1,000 feet above the water and still descending. However, this time it wasn't the virus making them fall but the engines slowly dying from the strain.

In the distance, Michael could make out the coastline of Myrtle Beach rapidly approaching.

They couldn't attempt a landing at the airfield; they would certainly hit the tops of the nearest hotels before ever getting close to the runway. As Michael told Aron this, they both knew there was only one option left.

"Michael, you need to make a water landing! Lower your tail so it hits the water first!"

Michael understood, and did as he was instructed.

BENEDICT, JUST OUTSIDE THE COCKPIT, TRIED NOT TO BE AMONG THE SCREAMING PASSENGERS, THOUGH HE WAS TEMPTED TO JOIN THEM AS THE PLANE LURCHED UP.

He tried to remain as calm as possible, confident that they would all get out of this. But in the confusion, he noticed something out of place.

At the end of the cabin stood a young boy. He had dark blond hair and wore a brown leather jacket and square glasses. Benedict committed the image to memory as the boy reached out to him.

Benedict returned the gesture, beckoning to the boy to come to the front of the cabin where he could be safe.

But he just stood there, a longing expression on his faraway face.

Then, he was gone as the back half of the plane slammed down. The empty cabin beyond where the boy had stood was ripped from the rest of the plane with a metallic screech before exploding in the ocean behind them.

Finally, Benedict screamed.

MICHAEL FOUGHT TO SLOW THE PLANE DOWN, NEVER REALIZING THAT HE HAD JUST LOST THE WHOLE BACK HALF. He pushed

buttons that did nothing, the wings and part of the upper hull having been ripped from the aircraft by the initial impact. Part of the first-class cabin was now exposed to the night sky, as was the occupied coach compartment.

They were nearing the beach rapidly, momentum propelling what remained of the fuselage forward. Then, for the first time in the flight, they began to noticeably slow, their impact further muffled by the sand bars ahead.

Along the quiet, deserted beach, the fuselage did no harm as it made land, finally stopping with what remained of the back half barely touching the waterline, listing slightly to the left.

SILENCE FILLED THE PHONE LINE FOR WHAT SEEMED LIKE AN ETERNITY.

The group in Networking Hub 17 waited anxiously for someone on the other end to say something. Eventually, even Nelson couldn't take any more.

"Michael, are you guys all right?" he asked through the headset.

Nothing.

"Michael, say something and let us know you're okay!" Aron yelled.

"Please!" Andrea added, close to tears.

Still nothing.

Then, as they began to give up hope, there was rustling on the other end. Someone was picking up the phone. They heard heavy, exhausted breathing as whoever it was pressed the phone to their ear.

"I'm sorry, but Michael had a sudden appointment with last night's dinner and a paper bag. Can I be of any assistance?"

For the first time in his life, one of Benedict's tasteless jokes was met with applause from Nelson and everyone else gathered in Networking Hub 17.

62

Friday, August 1st
Hampton Inn & Suites
Myrtle Beach, South Carolina
5:46 PM (Eastern Time)

Michael Ridding, National Hero.

Or so the media reported.

To the world's surprise, Michael had managed to save everyone onboard. Of course, he'd had help, but, as always, the others were happily left out of the spotlight.

Still, the news networks had been able to gather some information on the lone pilot. Never mind the crew and the strange man in the wool coat who had helped them to the front of the plane; one face looked better than several on the front cover of newspapers and magazines.

The situation was explained away as a power issue that had led to a decrease in oxygen in the cabin, killing the pilots before they had a chance to alert anyone. In the efforts to take control, the plane had been difficult for the first-time pilot to handle, but this brave hero had done as well as could be expected.

The crew was sworn to secrecy. Most were willing to go along with the cover story, given the funds Benedict provided. It would prove to be only a temporary solution, but it was the only one they had.

Besides, they believed the virus in its original form had died at Nelson's hand. And if not, he was hard at work on a program for flight computers that would act as a line of defense against similar attacks. It would be secretly installed over the course of several weeks as aircraft were taken in for maintenance, hopefully eliminating further threats.

The survivors had been met by emergency vehicles shortly after what was left of the plane came to rest on the beach. Everyone who needed to be treated was cared for on-site, only a few requiring a trip to the hospital.

News crew after news crew showed up next, eager to speak with the hero and get an exclusive interview. Even President Robinson wanted to extend his gratitude in person when the opportunity came. But, for Michael, it wasn't so simple to give in to everyone's praise.

He spent that night in Myrtle Beach, a view of the crash site visible from his hotel balcony, where he wrote a small statement for Benedict to post on the Internet somewhere that people could find it:

"I want to thank everyone for their kind words. I do not wish to come across as rude in not taking interviews, but I must decline all offers at this time. I have had an incredibly stressful time and I am looking forward to a hot shower and a good night's sleep. Once I feel I can be useful enough to take interviews, I will be more than happy to do so. For the moment, there's not much I can talk about that hasn't

already become public knowledge. I hope everyone understands this and knows that I am grateful, but I am even more grateful for the people who helped guide the plane down and that, by some miracle, we were able to save everyone on board."

-Michael Ridding

Michael was left alone, apart from several calls from family. And though he knew things were still rocky between him and his parents, he could tell that they were both glad he was safe.

Shortly after the letter was posted online, the flood of media attention slowed to a trickle. Within the week, he had no doubt they would go back to covering tabloid stories and shady politics. That was okay with him.

Being alive was enough for now.

63

Saturday, August 2nd
Palm Springs International Airport
Palm Springs, California
6:27 PM

BENEDICT FOUND THEM A PRIVATE JET FOR THE FLIGHT BACK HOME. It wasn't as fast or as nice as the *Bluestream*, but it did what it needed to.

Michael and Benedict left the crash site and what they hoped would be their last memory of Von Gord's family behind. They flew to Palm Springs, planning to drop Michael off before Benedict went on to a meeting in Las Vegas. Given all they had been through, Benedict had said he was far from in the mood for big business. But duty called, and he couldn't cancel this time.

The flight went by rather quickly, Michael and Benedict filling the time going over the future of their arrangement. While there were still hints of tension between them, neither felt that it would hinder their working relationship. And, to an extent, Michael understood that some secrets weren't ready to be unveiled.

But that didn't mean they wouldn't eat away at him.

They arrived in Palm Springs in the early evening.

Looking out over the expansive desert oasis as they touched down, Michael found it hard to believe he was home. He was about to see Granger, Aron, and Andrea again after what felt like forever but had actually been less than a week.

"So, now what?" Michael asked Benedict as the plane taxied down the runway. "Where do we go from here?"

Benedict looked at his friend. "If I have my way, I won't be doing anything for a while unless something comes up, since Las Vegas shouldn't be much of a meeting. There might be a trip this winter, but that's a long way off, ya know?"

These were the most welcome words Michael had heard in days.

Over the next few months, he would take things slow. No investigations, no strenuous work. He would finally have the time to relax, and he would take as much of it as he could.

But when Benedict needed him, he would be there.

The plane came to a stop near the *Bluestream*'s hangar. Outside the fence, they saw Aron standing by the exit, the Pantera not far away.

Now, Michael believed it.

He was home.

"Well, we'll see," Michael said as he extended his hand. "Thank you, Benedict. I know I should've said it before, but thank you for being honest with us and for giving me the chance to hopefully do some good."

Benedict firmly returned the handshake. "It's my

pleasure, Michael. And someday, I hope we can both understand all this. But not today. Today, we rest."

Michael exited the plane, heading for the Pantera with his new coat blowing in the cooling desert wind. He turned back to wave a final goodbye, but the plane was already heading for the runway.

Michael stood and watched as the strangest man he had ever met flew off and disappeared into the crimson sky.

Epilogue

Saturday, August 2nd
McCarran International Airport
Las Vegas, Nevada
7:44 PM

BENEDICT MADE HIS CONNECTION IN NEVADA, TRADING IN THE SMALL PRIVATE JET FOR A LARGE COMMERCIAL AIRPLANE. Although he always preferred the smaller, more nimble aircraft, he knew he couldn't trust pilots outside DenCom's influence to keep a secret.

The aircraft he met, with its all-white paint job and single red stripe down the windows, was one of only a handful in the world, and it was something of a mystery to everyone but those who lived and worked in Vegas. No one would have expected the small fleet's path, which only consisted of two destinations.

One was Las Vegas. The other was Dreamland.

Or so Benedict called it.

As he exited the small private jet and made the short walk to his connection, he made eye contact with a man he'd feared wouldn't show up.

President Jeffrey Robinson stood in the aircraft doorway, staring the smaller man down as he walked up the attached stairs.

Benedict reached the top and extended a hand. "Didn't expect to see you."

"I could say the same for you," Robinson replied with a look of contempt in his eyes.

It was a look Benedict knew he deserved. He had acted recklessly, both concerning the Von Gord affair and something else he knew the President was more interested in.

The door quickly shut behind them as they entered the massive plane together. The cabin was empty, except for one lone form Benedict easily picked out in the back.

"Talk with him for a while. But once we land, you and I need to have a chat," Robinson said as he took one of the front seats.

Ignoring the President's irritation with their guest, Benedict hurried to the rear of the plane, where he found the tall, thin man sitting in the last window seat to the left, looking down at a darkened tablet.

"Nelson? What are you—?"

"You need to see this." Nelson produced a white envelope from his coat pocket, not bothering to look up. "You remember the security alerts in your room?"

Benedict nodded.

"There was... there was a second signature," Nelson explained. "It showed up out of nowhere, and when it did, he... the first one fled, the sensors glitching again, this time acting like something was running down the stairs. This time, I... After the second signature disappeared, I decided to go over and investigate on my own, and... I found this on your bed. I opened it first, just to be sure there wasn't anything harmful inside... but there's more. Please, sit."

Benedict sat next to him as the plane began to move, hurrying toward the nearest runway. He took the envelope as the aircraft readied for takeoff, and the engines powered up as he removed the folded piece of paper.

The smell of garlic assaulted him as he caught a small, white object that floated out of the note with his free hand before it went numb.

That was a fun show.
I'll let your disobedience go. For now.
<u>*Do not test me further.*</u>

-M.P.

He let the note fall to his lap, gravity pressing it down as the plane took off.

Benedict opened his hand to see a small, white flower that had been crushed by the envelope. He looked it over.

"Joshua tree," Nelson confirmed, and the fear that struck Benedict made him want to jump out of the plane and let the engines mutilate him.

While Benedict contemplated his death, Nelson had turned on the tablet. Benedict looked at the image on the screen, sparking yet another suppressed urge to end his suffering before it could begin.

"This is from your security camera in the hallway," Nelson said. "It showed up right as the alerts quit coming in."

Benedict's stomach churned as he looked upon the young boy's face, his dark blond hair, square glasses, and forlorn expression unmistakable.

In that instant, he knew that some cosmic clock had just begun counting down to his destruction.

And yet, what truly terrified him was that he had no idea who he was looking at.

Even he didn't know everything, after all.

DURING THE SHORT FLIGHT, BENEDICT HAD DONE HIS BEST TO PUT ON A CALM DISPOSITION.

Soon after they landed in the dark airfield, they were met by a troop transport truck that would take them directly to DenCom's hangar.

It had taken a lot of pushing and prodding, not to mention favors, to build a hangar here, given Benedict's background and possible ulterior motives. But he knew that this was no "hotspot", no place for aliens to come and go as they pleased. Homey Airport was just a simple testing site for advanced, classified aircraft.

Still, Benedict couldn't deny that he had brought one of the most famous stereotypes to life.

He and the President were shown into the building while Nelson stayed on the plane. Benedict knew that Nelson would never set foot here again, which was something he had to respect. Years ago, the times had been different, and the guidelines of what made humans human had not been in Nelson's favor.

They headed for the elevator that would take them to the hangar's conference and viewing room. It hadn't been long since Benedict's last visit, but he felt it would be a good idea to check in on one of his bigger projects. Although he hadn't expected Robinson to come with him, he was not about to deny the Commander-in-chief his rightful place.

As the doors parted and both men entered, they were saluted by Dodgson until the President gave him permission to stand easy.

"Where are the Knights?" Benedict asked, seeing empty chairs lining the table.

"Down there," Dodgson replied, pointing out the viewing window. "The repair team's having issues with the reactor again."

Benedict nodded. He should have expected it.

It kept acting up. The reactor was temperamental at best, the stealth tech would occasionally fail without warning, and now, the sensors had supposedly given them faulty readings. The assault on Von Gord's compound might have been the first time things had gone smoothly, or so they'd thought until the most recent issue surfaced. The big question was whether or not it was worth further investigation. Checks had already been carried out since the assault with no sign of error, so they needed to decide if they could risk grounding the craft for several more weeks, maybe even months for a full check-up. And it didn't help that all this was coming down right when Robinson decided to pop in.

Benedict shouldn't have been surprised that the President wanted to check in on the project, but that was no easy task. There could be no security except what Homey provided, often leaving the President feeling nervous, even while visiting one of the most well-protected places in the world.

As they waited, Robinson sat at the head of the table, and Benedict looked out at their glorious creation.

In the sparsely lit hangar, the black hulking form could be seen among the occasional flying sparks from workmen.

It was the greatest feat thus far in the ongoing U.S. and DenCom collaboration, and Benedict still considered it to be his best contribution to date. Although Robinson had all but abandoned it in favor of a newer model, which made Benedict feel like a recently single parent, he couldn't deny that the President still had a strong interest in the project.

But he figured, like most things, that Robinson's tastes would shift as soon as the newer model came out.

However, the possibility of its successor being completed before the end of Robinson's second term was easily a fifty-fifty shot. At least they could both appreciate what lay before them today.

The craft was massive, its three-hundred-foot disc barely able to fit in the hangar. It was a marvel, a true feat of human technology. In most senses of the word, the thing was alien, but its heart was truly human, the greatest mechanical wonder yet to be constructed by man, even if it was already overshadowed by the forthcoming advanced model.

Eventually, craft like it would usher in a new age of travel. But the military wanted it first, as they did most things. And, as such, it was weaponized and fully capable as a dual-terrain vehicle, a strategist's dream come true.

It would be ready when the war came, but not without its flaws.

And it would be ready when Benedict needed it once again.

Coda:
The Valley Burns

THE SEAS OFF ANTARCTICA WERE STRANGELY CALM ON THIS DAY, DURING WHICH THE SUN WOULD NOT SET.

Gentle waves crashed against the hull of a rusted old ship. Dark red with a gargoyle-like face painted in black on the three-story superstructure, the ship would stand out to anyone who saw it floating among the treacherous ocean waters. Yet, those few who caught even a glimpse were never able to catch up with it; the ship always slipped away, speeding off into the oblivion that was the Antarctic Ocean.

On either side of the bow, the name of its owner was painted in black. The name itself, however mundane or disappointing, was never spoken aloud outside the ship. There was a time and a place for it to be spoken, and this was neither.

Below deck, two women sat alone in a dark room, lit only by the candles on the floor in the shape of a defaced pentagram, its nature of no importance at this time. The two women, against their wishes, were reluctantly significant now.

The first, a young redhead, sat in a viewing chair as her companion meditated. She was thin, yet strong and attractive. Her hair flowed gracefully at her sides, shimmering in the candlelight, the same rusty hue as the ship around them.

The second woman, or man, as it were, sat across from the redhead in a deep meditation. During this time, she would speak and breathe sparingly, hoping to make some sense out of the cosmic nightmare around her. Her face was bony, the result of her male features attempting to defile her preferred feminine appearance. Black, unkempt hair draped from her shoulders in clumps, just waiting for her to lean in too close over the candles and end their hideous lives.

Her eyebrows raised, she was tuned into whatever consciousness wanted them to know more about their predicament.

"He is active," the black-haired woman said, never wavering from her stance. "Very active, in fact."

"What does it mean?" the redhead asked, desperate for answers.

"It means… he is still there, but he is not ready." She took in another deep breath.

"Are they dead, my family?" the redhead asked. She saw the black-haired woman shift in her stance. Not a good sign.

"I do not see them," she replied flatly.

The redhead leaned back and sighed, unable to contain her disappointment. "We have to go to Benedict. We don't have much time."

The black-haired woman opened her eyes, the trance still active within her, universal thought pouring through her body, or so she claimed. "We have five years at best. It is enough. We can wait."

"But if we talk to him, then—"

"Nothing will change if we do it now," the black-haired woman said, the trance coming to a gentle end. "He is not ready for us. We both know that. We must take our time and wait until the perfect moment to confront him."

The redhead took this in, having heard the speech before. The black-haired woman sighed as well, her personality returning. They stared at the symbol between them, the candles slowly dimming as wax fell away.

"We're going through with this, aren't we?" the redhead asked.

She always asked, but only to the other woman. They had known each other for years, had been friends since the days when all this was nothing more than a dream. To the rest of the small crew, she would keep her strong yet open face from showing any mistrust, any fear of what her husband had planned so long ago.

But here, with her friend, she could be honest.

"Yes," she replied. "We are going forward. And if you need any other reason, remember that this has been part of you from conception. No matter what happens now, we have started something that needs to be finished, no matter the cost. We might sacrifice our sanity, even our lives, but we will see it done."

With that, the last of the candles faded away, taking the two women with them. They would retreat again, back among the forgotten, into the shadows, waiting for the day they would cure the world.

"SOME THINGS ARE ALWAYS KEPT FROM THE BEST OF US. Such things I know I can find with your help. And such things, those that you want to know, cannot be exposed without me. For without me, you are nothing. You are a waste of the world's time, a waste to those you love.

"And I, being so humble, can give you this choice to go on, to come with me down a path that could kill any and all of your remaining morals, those that hide in the corners of your mind, screaming out in meek, high-pitched voices, begging to be heard. I will help bring them under your heel. I will help you become something you hate.

"And if you choose not to join me, I will hand you the gun that will end your life.

"And I will laugh as what's left of you spills out onto the Valley floor, your blood feeding all that I am, all that I ever wanted to be.

"And I will take what little joy you leave behind with me to Hell."

-M.P.
Welcome Home.

WE

ALSO FROM PROJECT 89 MEDIA

questionMark by Faryl

Six bizarre stories:
Grotesque, enchanting,
and everything in between

The experience is unpredictable,
so what will happen when you read?

AVAILABLE NOW ON AMAZON IN EBOOK, PAPERBACK, AND AUDIOBOOK

53308771R00190

Made in the USA
Lexington, KY
29 September 2019